Mito-Samhita

Use the knowledge of mitochondria to manifest health

Avishek Mukhopadhyay

Copyright © <2024> <Avishek Mukhopadhyay>

Contents:

Introduction

This book is my understanding of the mitochondria put into a compressed and easy to understand version. While writing it I kept reminding myself that the person going to read it would not be interested in knowledge of complicated biological functions to flex it in the next tea party, instead a person who is hungry to get his life back on track. Because I am that person too. The knowledge here is inspired from my favourite go-to books about mitochondria. Another reason for writing this book is to make this knowledge available to people who find it very costly to buy western books which costs few thousand bucks when bought in India. I just hope I could help few people by acting as a channel to allow this knowledge to trickle down to more people. Together we can counteract the empire of commercial forces which are blind to human health hazards while focussing solely on profits (the telecommunication and pharma giants). Please go ahead and absorb this book, if you feel a topic is touched too briefly in this compressed work, feel free to research & expand on the topic yourself.

Mitochondria enthusiasts know & understand health best

For human health, biophysics is far more important than diet, exercise, genes, toxins, microbiome, and leaky gut.

That's because of the golden rule of modern wellness which says "until you stop staying in the environment that made you sick, you won't get well fully", but almost everyone ignores it.

Light, water & magnetism are the physical forces that control mitochondria & biorhythms which in turn determine our health.

All other things like diet, supplements, exercising, work as assistants to the above primary three factors and will give you little or temporary gains unless the main factors are in place.

Around the 70s medical world became overconfident since it could treat symptoms successfully. Realizing its futility people started going after natural healing like gut microbiome, exercising, detox etc but this was also not enough ! As we advance more in wireless technology, there is another important dimension of our health which we can sense but the west denies.

Doctors & natural healers believe biochemistry is the answer, that our chemical imbalance causes disease. But biochemistry is ruled by photoelectricity which power plants & animals.

Light frequencies (visible/invisible), water & magnetism control our biology. All our signalling molecules, metabolism, cognitive function, sleep, and anti-aging efforts are subordinate to light, water, magnetism & electromagnetic frequencies (good/bad).

ATP(energy) is made in a mitochondria by an "electron transport chain" (ETC) not a protein, carbohydrate or fat transport chain. Body chemistry works by electrons, protons & photons, not by protein, carbs or fats.

We have always made the mistake of going after & suppressing symptoms, now we will discover how biophysics hits the very root of the problems.

For long the elites of the world had us believe that they are genetically superior and hence elite. In other words, 'genes decide our fate' is what we have been fed. Thus in a way justifying the differences in health, wealth & better life that they have. But we will now understand how its not genes but environment that affect our mitochondria & circadian rhythms and thus govern our entire life, physical, intellectual & success in life.

Druggists, doctors & healers made us think from a "deficiency-additive" perspective which says we 'lack' something and hence to be healthy we have to 'take' something in. But we should focus on just removing the obstacles and let the body heal and rebalance itself. Finally we need to reconnect to the best & original healing and wellness support, called Nature.

Diet, exercise etc always occupied our attention because with them the cause & effect are easier to see. People ignore forces of physics and don't act until health starts failing. Here you will learn the answers to the problems which frustrated generation after generation:

> Loosing weight & keeping it off
> Feeling tired all the time
> Focus & attention span of kids
> 25% of women taking anti-depressant or anti-anxiety drugs
> People have insulin resistance & diabetes, why?
> Why so much infertility among couples?

Doctors will never tell you that improvement of internal energy production will rid you of common or complex diseases. So welcome to mitophysics, the science of mitochondria and circadian rhythms. It tells us how friendly electromagnetic frequencies, pure water & earth's magnetic field give us life, energy and disease-resisting power. Conversely foreign frequencies, impure water & non uniform magnetic fields deplete us.

Few examples of mitophysics in action:

- Plant use photons from sun and produce sugar & energy.
- Mitochondria use photon, electron & protons to power our biology.
- UV & IR light heals and regenerates us via receptors in our eye, skin, gut & fat.
- Blue light wakes us up by turning on our hormone production stress response.
- Water has a "fourth phase" where it becomes a battery(H+ & O-) which cells use.
- Body uses "para-magnetism" to transport blood, hormones, oxygen & DHA — and to re-condense & regroup proteins after a day's work.
- Our infradian rhythms (annual cycles) syncs to the seasons by exposure to light, food & temperature.

Mitophysical challenges that we face today:

- Inefficient & weak mitochondria makes us eat more and retain more calories in order to have enough energy to run the body
- Newly found hormone 'Leptin' regulates the production & expenditure of our energy. Functions like adrenal, immune, insulin signalling, fertility, even our emotion are under its ambit. Lack of leptin sensitivity is reason behind failure to loose weight.

- ➢ Eating out-of-season fruits & veggies affect mitochondria & causes weight gain, disease & premature aging. It results in deuterium ('heavy water' – h2o with 1 extra neutron) accumulation in our system.
- ➢ Artificial blue light disturbs our biorhythms, depletes neurotransmitters, causes hormone problems, sleep disturbance & adrenal issues.
- ➢ Grounding/earthing gives you energy to heal.
- ➢ Non-native EMF frequencies upsets human health in a big way.

Neglecting these things affect the health which people try to desperately compensate by good food & supplements. Children having insulin resistance, 95% women autoimmune to her own thyroid, teenagers getting arthritis, osteoporosis or cancer, 1 in 35 children having autism are all warning signs.

Body is not the problem, environment is! We are always looking inside when something's wrong, we do blood work, MRI etc, not knowing these are just distress signals, not the source. Physical symptoms are just the downstream consequences of our light, magnetism & water's effect on our mitochondria & circadian rhythms. 80-90% diseases are due to mitochondria, only 5-20% are primarily genetic. Mitochondria are more responsive to environment than DNA.

When light slows down, things having mass show up. This principle is used by our bodies to make various biochemicals. For example sunlight hits certain amino acids in the eye to make dopamine, melatonin, serotonin etc. Digestion releases light from food. Sunlight makes POMC in hypothalamus which further creates beta-endorphins (which makes us feel good in the sun) and ACTH(precursor of cortisol) but beta endorphin is the only non addictive opioid that doesn't increase cravings.

Eye contains many amino acids which combines with sunlight to make neurotransmitters.

The entire energy creation of the planet comes from the sun.

The one size fits all approach is coming to an end in medical field, now everyone should be treated individually. Biochemistry as an effect of biophysics are varied across populations. Western medicine is now less reliable since last 20-30 years, mainly after the advent of glyphosate(weed killer) & wireless communication.

Sunlight on eyes and skin determines healing, hormone levels & mitochondrial output. Same applies for DHA(fatty acid) in diet, non native EMF, deuterium levels in water & magnetic environment(where one lives).

Group studies and results are also less reliable because they are often done in hospital under blue light. For instance testing an water purifier only on Japanese people to get a conclusion, who eat more seafood resulting in more DHA in them and hence successful in converting more sunlight into energy.

A new concept called "n=1" is being accepted more & more among mitochondria nerds. Here 'n' means "you are your own subject" and should be treated like a unique case acc. to your mitochondrial efficiency.

Its no more the old times of pre 4G & wifi when you had the time, lifestyle or bank account to casually approach a health problem where you would try a regimen, a guru's routine and then try another when the former doesn't give result. At present if you neglect your health, you will have to pay for it, as simple as that. All because of unfriendly biophysical forces. We have to bring the friendly physical forces back to our lives if we want to have a chance at healing.

Exemplary health in a 5G world will take some effort. Being healthy is no more an entertainment, it's a journey. Now it's the survival of the best-educated, most proactive & fully committed.

Mitophysics is multi-layered, you will get many options to improve yourself. You can add many principles, practices & products to your routine. Establishment kept away this knowledge from medical field for 100 years. Biophysics is the answer.

Before electrification all our mitophysical environment were almost same, hence there was less variations in results. World is becoming n=1 slowly, pay attention to the clues you are getting from your body, that's the real feedback. That's what a mitochondria enthusiast really works with.

Away from nature, into the matrix

We are meant to live in harmony with nature, not technology. Which means:

> Eyes & skin getting sun at the right time.
> Direct body contact with the earth
> Drinking water from natural sources
> Locally grown food

These give power to our bodily functions and harmonize us with seasons.

But we suffer when we choose to detach from mother nature and tune in to manufactured technologies.

3.8 billion years ago earth was full of two kinds of organisms, bacteria & archaea.

650 million years ago plants struck a deal with archaea that it can stay in plants and in return it has to help plants turn sunlight into food. Today they are known as chloroplasts. As byproducts plants released oxygen and put DHA into the seas.

More Oxygen was produced from ozone and stronger sunlight(middle age of sun) and DHA helped produce electricity. DHA helped multi cellular organisms to harvest sunlight directly, allowing them to be in touch with sun & earth intermittently.

Again around 600 million years ago archaea made a deal with bacteria. Archaea would allow them to stay in them and eat their food but in return bacteria would have to change its genome so that it can digest the unmetabolized food of archaea into a form that it can metabolize. Those archaea became 'eukaryotes' & those bacteria became 'mitochondria'. The ultimate eukaryote is man. Genes are transferable from multiple mitochondria to a cell's nucleus, its advantageous. That's how multicelled organisms become more elaborate with time. Mitochondria focussed only on energy production and eukaryotes focussed on fancier things like:

> Building a brain
> Muscle, nerves & bones
> Making the system adaptive to environment

But since it all started in the sea(as mentioned earlier), water is still important to the cell, so mitochondria started to do the reverse of photosynthesis, turning food and oxygen into CO_2 and water.

The first circadian mismatch started when man started wearing clothes. Our skin is like a solar cell collecting and producing DC electricity. Its used in cellular activities which run and repair us. Luckily nature gives us backup energy source if we lack sunlight(more on that later).

Second mismatch is the discovery of fire. It was tremendously useful no doubt but it slowly reduced the body's need to produce its own heat. Mitochondria became weak by not exercising its thermal plasticity.

Finally in the 19th century man invented AC current, and from that started artificial light, artificial heat, rubber sole shoes, UV blocking glasses, sunscreen, fruits shipped in off-seasons, etc. Today wireless & 5G is everywhere, killing us literally. When shall we wake up from our blue lights, is the question.

Food is basically condensed sunlight because it was produced by photosynthesis.

Our mitochondria does the opposite, it converts food(sugar) and oxygen into CO_2 and water. Happy byproducts are energy(ATP) & light (infrared heat). Food electrons carry energy and information which are released inside our body.

Plants and animals are truly interdependent.

Einstein's photo electric effect says light falls on certain elements resulting in release of electrons. By logic it means that light interacts with electron, not proton or neutron. Light makes electrons spin in certain ways. Electrons of food retain that spin until our mitochondria reverses it by turning food into ATP in our cells. From those spin states, our mitochondria understands where that food was grown and how to accordingly control our metabolism. Mitochondria deciphers and converts those spins back into various light frequencies, mainly IR & UV. These lights energises respiratory proteins and helps create exclusion zone water(4th phase), which cells use to power its processes. This is why plants struggle to live outside its native place, but not animals. Chlorophyll and haemoglobin are structurally similar but former has a magnesium atom in its core while the later has an iron atom. Mg has 12 electrons while Fe has 26 electrons which can absorb light. So chlorophyll can absorb narrower band of frequencies, mainly blue and red. But animal blood can absorb broader spectrum of light including IR & UV. So animals can adapt in less than ideal light situations. In short, animals have a bigger and better storage tank of lights.

Health & light are interrelated

➢ By einstein eqn e=mc2 , light slows down to form matter

➢ Light mixes with CO2 and water to form all plant matter(source of all food chain)

Now lets see light and animal life:

➢ Eye, skin, gut & lungs have photoreceptors for capturing light. These 'opsins' activate our internal pharmacy to make hormones to control metabolism, sleep cycle & regeneration.
➢ Our cells store light when their surrounding water gets IR & visible light. Water turns into charge separated e-zones.
➢ DHA turns light into DC electricity (and back)
➢ Respiratory proteins inside mitochondria absorb light of one frequency and release light of another frequency. For ex: it absorbs light from food electrons and produces IR to heat up or shrink water around respiratory proteins.

Prokaryotes like bacteria(or archaea) don't have DHA in their cell membranes. They cant store light as fat, they can never become complex. They will always remain single celled.

Leakage of light is responsible for disease. When a cell is under stress, it emits a little amount of very low frequency UV light (ELF UV) also called biophotons. That stress can be physical injury, toxins, lack of nutrients, infection, environment, emotion(crying), orgasm, exertion. However these are not inherently harmful, rapid loss or slow replenishment is harmful. Ability to harvest, store & later use light is the hallmark of health.

One way we lose light is during unwinding of our DNA helix. It unwinds during protein synthesis so that cell may read the codes to make proteins. During the process photons need to be strongly held in place or they get lost as low frequency UV or IR(heat).

When light is lost, body also struggles to read light information from electrons. Food grown in strong sunlight may work against you if eaten in weak sunlight conditions.

Body part with weak mitochondria leaks energy, for instance an anorexic person loses light from brain, an obese person from liver & pancreas.

Electrons run our health as they turn the gear of ATP production. Lack of electrons produce positive charge, which results in acidity, inflammation, low voltage, dehydration and low regeneration of cells and mitochondria, leading to faster aging.

Four sources of electrons:

- Food
- Sun exposure
- Grounding
- Burning stored fat

Energy yield from those electrons are then governed by

> ➢ Water quality/quantity
> ➢ Tightness of mitochondrial protein packing

Plants can get electrons from earth 24/7 and they have foliage to get photons from sun. They are like all time plugged batteries, always grounded. So they don't need to eat food and store fat.

But humans are made to be unplugged and mobile:

> ➢ We can have 2nd hand energy by eating plants
> ➢ We can have 3rd hand energy by eating animals that ate plants
> ➢ We can convert our own stored fat back to energy
> ➢ We can get electron by grounding & sun exposure
> ➢ We can also charge our mammalian battery by exposure to native light frequencies

(mammalian battery = energy store for cells. Ex: ezone, ATP chemical bonds, cell membrane, energy from bone-ligament-tendon by muscle movement, spiralling cosmic energy in DNA called 'scalar energy')

Bottom line: fat, carb & proteins are just containers of sun energy. When we eat them our mitochondria release those energy as electron, proton and light. If you get doses of electron from nature, you need less food & you are less hungry. Its easier to lose weight, you take less sugar and so your insulin burden is less too.

So for better use of electrons:

> Better hydration
> Better grounding
> Getting more sun
> Increase mitochondrial efficiency (eg: cold thermogenesis)

This will lessen dependence on food so extra weight and diabetes will go away. Modern lifestyle is draining away all electrons from our lives, plus we are closing the chances of recovery by leaning too much on technology. Our mistakes are:

> Not getting direct sun exposure
> Not touching earth directly
> Not drinking pure water
> Not eating seasonal, whole food

Modern living causes inflammation & oxidative stress. When persistent they consume even more electrons which could be used to look younger or feeling better. Blue light, 4G, 5G, fluoridated water, & processed food drain lots of electrons.

> Non native EMFs drain electron from our tissues & oscillate mitochondria at such a frequency that impairs fat burning and ATP production.
> Fluoridated & chlorinated water reduces the ability of water to separate into H-positive and OH-negative ions so water cant store more energy(e-zone water)

- ➢ Processed high-carb food are more acidic as they lose electrons during processing. Whole food has more electrons
- ➢ Moving air steals electrons, so we get tired after long sleep under fan, ac, long bike ride etc. Skin should be covered during such activities.

Darwin was misunderstood, he never said that life evolves out of random mutation & natural selection. His work (some claim not his own) was changed in 1871. In his original work of 1859 he said "conditions of existence are far more important than natural selection". So it basically means life changes genetic expression according to environment, not random accidents.

It happens through epigenetics. Basically environment changes our mitochondria and that mitochondria is then passed on from mother to children. Characteristics like skin tone, constitution, metabolism, body shape, longevity etc seem to evolve through generations for this reason.

Cycles of seasons

Why does animals in cold places don't catch cold? Its not because of fur or feathers. They have mechanism to produce more heat which in turn is retained better by fur, fat, etc.

Their mitochondria crank up heat during winter by burning more brown fat. More precisely it's the dwindling UV light in late fall sunlight that falls on eye, skin, gut that triggers this heat production, not winter exactly. Grounding also helps in electron gain. Grounding thins the blood and doesn't let it stick together thus helps to keep warmer. Can man also enjoy same benefit ? lets see...

Modern man never faced proper winter. If we always stay in heated atmosphere in winters, slowly our mitochondrial fortitude atrophies. Many people lost seasonal temperature variability because mitochondria has become weak as it was never put into some hard work of producing own heat. More you expose to winter with less clothes, the more you will notice that you will not feel cold so overwhelming anymore. But that's not the only benefit, your mitochondria will be younger & fit. So don't let mitochondria be lazy.

Out of season foods make you pay biological toll...

The west especially gets fruits and vegetables shipped from distant countries to enjoy in winter. But it doesn't mean we should do it. Nature planned our metabolism around light cycles. Fruits, vegetables & carbs are for summer when sun emits lots of UV but in winter they detune the mitochondria and promote weight gain. Summer programming is designed not to store fat as you are expected to be more active. So high calorie is balanced by more UV released from food, which minimizes fat storage and charges up the bodily water. Similarly when we eat fruits in winter, it erodes mitochondrial functions especially when we avoid cold on top of wrong food. Notice how our craving for fruit goes down when it gets cold, and increases when its hot as the photonic energy in fruit is matched with your environment(latitude, altitude, cloud cover, temperature). Seasonal switch is activated by UV light hitting our eyes and skin. Weak UV makes us gain weight in winter and vice versa.

Off season food causes photoelectric mismatch. Adding fuel to fire are processed foods with refined sugar which amplifies the effects.

Tropical fruits are made of intense light of equator where chlorophyll-A is present. But plants in higher latitudes with weaker sunlight has chlorophyll-B so that they can capture high frequency UV light to make up for low sunlight. Accordingly biological programs are turned on in our body when the food gets digested and the photo receptors in our gut is hit by UV light of that particular food. These are some reasons of seasonal weight fluctuation.

There is however one factor which is not in our hands, its our "haplotype". Its racially inherited ancestral programming on how to metabolize our food like a baseline.

People are programmed to eat like their ancestors' native food habits. Haplotype is how loosely or tightly your mitochondria are coupled. For instance population from equator are designed to produce more ATP and less heat whereas Alaskan eskimos produce more heat, less ATP. Their main enemy is cold, not a chasing predator. So for example a northerner eating lots of tropical food will still not gain weight no matter where he currently lives but can suffer from metabolic problems like diabetes, inflammation as they are designed to make more heat than ATP.

The driver of our biological programming

Our eyes are much more than cameras, their functions are:

> - Decipher how much each wavelength of EM spectrum is present in sunlight including UV & IR
> - Inform the brain what time of day it is
> - Control daily & seasonal cycles, growth, metabolism, regeneration accordingly

When brain loses control of organs & systems we think its hormone imbalance. There is a pea sized part of brain known as 'suprachiasmatic nucleus' (SCN) which controls daily & seasonal cycles. It also controls:

> - Metabolism and its speed via leptin receptors
> - Sleep and recycling of mitochondria via melatonin
> - Fertility through testosterone & estrogen

Sadly SCN is faulty in people nowadays. There is a time keeping mechanism in the SCN and there is also a circadian clock gene in every cell through which the SCN controls the cell. The SCN clock runs milliseconds earlier so that the signal reaches the cell exactly on time (like hitting a moving target). If cell clock falls behind SCN-clock then there is imperfect synchronization, results are inflammation, disorder & disease. Bottom line: bio communication in body happens at light speed(new concept), not by chemicals(old concept).

Timing errors are caused by:

> Weak electric & magnetic field in SCN. Solution is DHA but blue light destroys it in the eye.
> Internal organs exposed to nnEMFs. For instance working with a tablet or laptop on your lap vibrates the lower abdomen and speeds up clock genes in reproductive organs faster than SCN. It looks like hormone imbalance and infertility occurs. Being under sunlight with lower body immersed in cold water cures it.
> Elevation is another reason. Every step away from ground level slows SCN little bit. Occasional flight passengers wont feel but pilots & crews are at more risk. Plane is like a microwave-irradiated metal tube. So moderation should be practiced.
> Space flight is worst reason, though most common people need not worry. People staying in high earth orbit just destroys circadian rhythm as a person is away from literally all the factors that tightly regulates biology.

Tissues and organs talk among themselves through 'entangled particles'(concept of physics). Biochemists believe it happens through chemicals or hormones but they are the secondary effect of something primary.

Glands talk to organs through free radicles and their once connected electrons. They maintain a distance bond which einstein called 'spooky action at a distance'. Connected at a quantum level. A free radical may stay in liver and its free electron might travel to the brain, now they are in communion through quantum entanglement. This is how brain keeps track of all organs, more entangled particles means better the working of that organ. When lack of free radicles happen glands loses touch with organs and chaos happens.

- Obesity: means brain lost coherence with liver and pancreas.
- Alzheimer's: SCN gets disconnected from brain but organs remain well connected.
- Infertility: leptin receptor & pituitary got disconnected from testes & ovaries.

Role of brain cells in waking or sleeping you: around 4am circadian system starts releasing cortisol in brain and body. This releases water in brain which expands neurons/cells and you wake up. Sunrise light starts the reverse process which finally ends during sunset(less blue - more red) after which melatonin starts getting produced. Melatonin rises into the evening, countering the effect of cortisol by calming you until sleep comes. Next day again same cycle.

Mitochondria & cell membrane are sensors. They collect energy information from outside and regulate our production of ATP, free radicles, body heat, metabolic water, magnetism & redox potential.

Mitochondria are sensitive to many stimuli

- Electron density: for instance fat, whole food have more electron while processed food have less, hence acidic. Mitochondria adjusts electron transport accordingly.
- Oxygen level: mitochondria are acutely aware of oxygen levels no matter what activity you are doing
- Water quality: low deuterium water helps store more energy
- Temperature: cold makes us burn brown fat and produce IR light.
- Red light: when absorbed by skin and released by mitochondria makes ATPase spin faster
- Magnetic flux: magnetism increases energy production from mitochondria

Mitochondria measures the efficiency of energy production through free radical signals. Blue light and nnEMF scramble the signals. Mitochondria becomes mis-tuned and produce less energy and more free radicals leading to disease.

Mitochondria harvests sun's energy. Just like chloroplast in plant absorb photon energy and its electrons jump to higher orbits and later released during respiratory chain, similarly mitochondria harvests photonic energy from food. Food is carrier of light for mitochondria.

Membranes act as electromagnetic antenna. Cell & mitochondria also sense how surrounding vibrations oscillate their surface, like electric/magnetic fields, food, water, drugs, even person to person vibes(biophotons).

- ➢ Voltage gated calcium channels: these channels on cell membrane detect tiny electric current and pass information back & forth.
- ➢ Oscillation in inner mitochondrial membrane: respiratory complexes generally vibrate at 100Hz, electric power grid vibrate at 50Hz which is its second harmonic. Thats how they complicate mitochondria and disrupt fat & protein burning.

Beginning point of health & sickness is mitochondria

65 million years ago Chicxulub asteroid hit earth and because of its debris earth went into almost 100 years of sun block & photosynthesis block. Only two creatures survived, flying dinosaurs & mammals that hibernate. Both have larger mitochondrial tanks to store huge energy. Remnant of that trait is ketosis and renewal during sleep, that's why sleep is so important. It repairs cells, balances biochemicals & renews mitochondria.

Mitochondria makes:

➢ deuterium depleted water which is best for us
➢ Generates magnetism
➢ Produce redox potential
➢ They are environmental sensors
➢ Makes ATP

Mitochondria population weaken

➢ With age
➢ When toxin & disease mutate their dna
➢ Lack of sleep & exercise
➢ When their communication network breakdown

➢ You are malnourished

Biologists think ATP is energy carrying molecules, but its not fully true. It also unfolds proteins to expose their binding sites to water. Then proteins function correctly & water also(in a special form) provides power to the cell. Cells supported by that kind of water is now known as 'e-zone' or exclusion zone. This charge differential gives cells the DC electricity they need. So ATP helps in forming such e-zones. Food should give us 1/3 of required ATP, 2/3 should come from sunlight, e-zone & grounding.

Oxygen for us is the taxi carriers that accepts the electrons coming out of a process called electron transport chain(ETC) and carries them away safely, so that harmful free radicals are not formed.

Reactive oxygen species(free radicals) is like smoke from fire, signifying imbalance in electron transport chain. One of its effects is when you have inflammation after consuming refined oil which is produced in huge sunlight but your eyes are signalling to your body that its fall or winter.

Its normal for mitochondria to become weak in old age but nowadays young people are also getting it, even some babies got dead mitochondria in the womb. When mitochondria malfunctions, cells resort to emergency mechanism of staying alive on sugar. This manifests as sugar and carb cravings, resulting in gluten sensitivity & candida overgrowth.

Mitochondrial genes of a person's ethnic lineage is called his "haplotype". It comes from the part of the planet the women in his family came from.

Bad human gene don't cause disease, bad/defective mitochondrial gene does. Disease is caused by weak mitochondria which then influence epigenetic changes upon our own gene expression. Cancer research is also wrongly focussed on genome rather than mitochondria, instead of studying already damaged gene, the mitochondria should be studied to know why the cancer came on the first place.

Autophagy: recycling of mitochondria:

Called mitophagy in case of mitochondria, it's the controlled breakdown of cells so its contents can be recycled & reused. It requires:

> Good sleep
> Intermittent fasting
> Regular exercise
> Electron flow
> Magnetic field
> Controlled production of free radicals

Free radicals are used to breakdown old worn out mitochondria, to make room for new ones. But with reduced electric & magnetic field, oxygen cant be held in place to remove an electron and hence less free radicals are produced and autophagy suffers. That's why long term ketosis without any carbs is useless. Carbs help supply the superoxides.

Apoptosis: it means programmed cell suicide. ATP also help mitochondria in controlled self destruction. Botton line, even the expiration of old mitochondria requires energy.

Heat shock protein 70: when northern descent people get cold stress(or heat stress), HSP 70 is

33

released. It stabilizes shape & size of protein in mitochondria so that respiratory complexes stay same. This minimizes heteroplasmy, ATP loss, excess free radicals. Bottom line: if you never allow yourself to get cold(or particularly hot), you lose this protective programming.

Mitochondria can convert light of one wavelength to another. It acts like a mini sun inside the cell to support cellular work. Things that offset this:

- Non native EMFs: blue light and microwaves
- Statins: cholesterol lowering drugs
- Antibiotics: mitochondria is evolved bacteria, so it is also affected
- Smoking
- Anti inflammatories & pain killers
- Anti anxiety drugs (Valium/Xanax)
- Anti depressants
- Anti psychotics
- Artificial colours: example – blue colour in candy & shaving gel affects ETC

We are also acting against mitochondria by:

- Non stop wifi & cell phone signals
- Circadian mismatch of artificial light & avoiding seasonal temperature change
- Processed food, high carb diet, deuterium bomb fruits, fluoride in water
- Lack of real sun exposure & direct earth contact

Rejuvenating the mitochondria:

> - Get full spectrum sun: IR & UV make more ATP
> - Reduce stress level
> - Make more melatonin: take more UV light in eyes from sun
> - Avoid nnEMFs: cut non native EMFs, especially blur light, wireless network
> - Drink good water: not fluoridated or chlorinated, free from deuterium
> - Deuterium free food: eat in-season fruits, avoid processed food, carbs, oils
> - Get cold exposure: purposely get cold occasionally(under-dress or cold bath)
> - Avoid mito-toxins: statins, antibiotics, cigarette
> - Take supplements: D-ribose & CoQ10 supplements good for mitochondria

Redox potential, inflammation & redox signalling

Communication is the key by which trillions of our body cells keep harmony with trillions of our gut microbiota. 3 main types of communication:

> - Neurotransmitters conduct signal along nerve path through dopamine & serotonin
> - Hormones regulate activity of organs from distance
> - DNA transmits genetic blueprint into protein making, cells & organisms.

Redox signalling: it's the communication that happens at a cellular level, made by mitochondria during cell respiration. The body uses this to:

> - Protect against foreign invaders & toxins
> - Detect damage and inform it to immune system
> - Repair cell when damage is reversible
> - Replace cell when damage is irreversible
> - Adjust energy production & metabolism
> - Adapt to seasonal changes

Redox molecules are both the communication network of the mitochondria, and the disinfectant that wipes out unwanted material to make way for new cells. Redox reactions and pH regulation both work to achieve electron balance. That's why raw, naturally produces vegetable is very good for us. Taking anti oxidant pills are not effective. Only 4% anti oxidants come from food, but internally produced 'glutathione' is about 85%. Exercise benefits the body by enhancing oxidation, reduction and redox signalling. By redox signalling body can:

- Detect when cells are stressed
- Tell DNA to start coping mechanism
- Activate immune system to fight threat
- Repair mildly damaged cell
- Regulate hormonal response
- Fine tune mitochondrial metabolism
- Turn off coping mechanism after threat is gone

Options for nucleus when it needs help:

- DNA repair option mobilizes dna repair crew
- Anti oxidant boost option makes surplus anti oxidants
- Intercellular communication option strengthens communication lines
- Increase blood supply option dilates blood vessels
- Stronger cell adhesion option makes inter cellular forces tighter
- Inflame tissue button stops damage from spreading
- Secrete antibiotics option produces own chemicals to fight invaders
- Stop cell division option stops damaged cell from replicating

- ➢ Send distress option sends signal to immune system
- ➢ More energy to repair option asks for more energy for repair works
- ➢ Prepare cell for shutdown option prepares to euthanize a cell
- ➢ Master shutdown option kills & demolishes a cell

When the last option(12th) malfunctions, weak cells replicate, and that called aging. Oxidative therapies use oxidation & reduction to heal:

- ➢ Hyperbaric oxygen chambers
- ➢ Chlorine dioxide
- ➢ Ozone therapy
- ➢ Hydrogen peroxide
- ➢ Exercise

When redox system fails:

- ➢ Slow cell repair
- ➢ Low energy
- ➢ Premature aging
- ➢ Immune system dysregulation
- ➢ Autoimmune problems
- ➢ Neurotransmitter & hormone imbalance
- ➢ Psychological disturbances
- ➢ Chronic inflammation

They take their toll as:

- ➢ Poor brain function in parkinson's, autism, ADD
- ➢ Irritable bowel syndrome, crohn's disease
- ➢ Insulin disfunction in diabetes

> ➢ Nerve damage in neuropathies
> ➢ Cardiac weakness in heart disease

Consuming sugar not only causes insulin production as per our old knowledge, it also causes mitochondria to produce more free radicals as by-product of ATP production. Eating lots of sugar and carbs is like pouring gasoline on fire. It's a sugar fuelled explosion of oxidation. This results in chronic inflammation and insulin flood in body.

Chronic inflammation drives degenerative diseases. It's the cause of problems of immune system, hormonal system, heart & brain problems, digestive tract and cell repair problems, basically everything in the body. Damage is not caused by pathogen but by the inflammation the body causes to fight it. Cancer is believed to take place after a cell has gone through 20,000 to 25,000 unrepaired damages to its DNA.

Inflammation can heal:

> ➢ Cuts, bruises, overuse injuries
> ➢ Damage to bones, muscles, tendons, internal organs, blood vessels
> ➢ Microbial infection
> ➢ Radiation damage
> ➢ Chemical/heavy metal poisoning
> ➢ Normal wear & tear

When there's an affected area, 1st stage inflammation kicks in and literally destroys anything it thinks foreign, then 2nd stage kicks in when rebuilding happens. When redox signalling is faulty, inflammation doesn't stop, both stages go on(creation & destruction) and that causes degenerative disease. Pain & swelling is important part of healing, if you avoid it by ice, compress, medication etc. your healing will be jeopardized.

Inflammation is of 2 types, acute(temporary & beneficial) and chronic(permanent & harmful). Its chronic when the immune system is unable to turn off the inflammation after its job is complete. Reasons for not turning off:

> Antioxidant system is overwhelmed, its when the inflammation is not strong enough to completely destroy the affected cells so they keep on replication in semi health condition and inflammation also keeps on in semi effectiveness until after years the inflammation becomes our enemy.
> Pro inflammatory situation sustains the situation, like eating pro inflammatory food(vegetable oil), leaky membranes, long term illness like lyme's disease, taking in toxins
> Less reductants, less redox signalling & shortage of energy prolong inflammation. With age we lose mitochondria, remaining mitochondria also age with us and also gets defective DNA just like our own DNA. They produce more oxidants and less reductants(lower redox potential). That's how chronic inflammation cause diseases be it heart, Alzheimer or diabetes.

Redox potential: its basically a function of how well we can convert sunlight, food & magnetism into DC electric charge while at the same time minimize losing electrons through modern living.

Negative charge/alkalinity = health

Positive charge/acidity = inflammation

Detox is a big term nowadays because of many toxins like mercury from sea food, chemicals like BPA and glyphosates, even extreme trauma like rape, abuse and armed combat make the brain hold onto heavy metals which are toxic. But detox should be viewed through the lens of redox. Detox is controlled by redox, which is a shotgun address to a wide range of issues, but detox is like rifle, only focussed on pinpoint problem, so bottom line: redox before you detox.

Earthing

It has the greatest health benefits, it gives oodles of vital resources to live, heal & resist aging, and that is electrons. Because of rubber soled shoe, artificial flooring or air conditioning we don't go out or don't get earthing. Its most effective way to get back redox potential. Its done by walking on bare earth without shoes or with specially designed conductive device from ground to your room. Disconnection may not kill you the next day but you heal slower, low energy, poor circulation, hormone imbalance, rapid aging, weight gain, mood off.

Benefits of earthing:

> - Donates electrons, rebuilds redox potential
> - It is like limitless antioxidants
> - Anti inflammatory
> - Natural blood thinner, so high pressure reduces, better circulation, oxygenation

And for these reasons earthing is found to:

> - Reduce chronic inflammation & its adverse effects
> - Decrease pain from variety of sources
> - Improve sleep in most people
> - Increase energy level
> - Reduce stress & promote calmness
> - Normalize body's biorhythms

- ➢ Reduce muscle tension & headaches
- ➢ Reduce hormonal & menstrual symptoms
- ➢ Speed healing & prevent bedsores
- ➢ Oppose jet lag
- ➢ Speed recovery from intense exercise
- ➢ Slow aging process

Grounding works better when sun is up, sun is positive anode & earth is negative cathode.

But using earthing devices has its problems, the house wiring picks up EMFs and dumps them in the earthing pin of the plug so using those devices connected to that pin can bring those dirty electrical imprints onto you. Better way is to stick a earthing rod in the ground and a dedicated wire connecting it to you separately. Lastly the very best way is always to go out and simply touch the ground with bare hands and feet, but with increase of 5G slowly that will also come with its problems.

Water's most important function

Water is the biggest mammalian battery. Water's most important contribution to human health comes from its electrical potential. The 4th phase of water is one of the most important discovery in the last century. Other names for it are:

> - Exclusion zone water
> - EZ
> - Structured water
> - Interfacial water
> - Charge separated water
> - H_3O_2
> - E-zone

Basically nature uses electrical charge to get things done whether by attraction or repulsion.

How the positive & negative charges in water separate? To power cellular work, ez water separates its charges and rearranges into hexagonal sheets, almost like an electrolyte. So water rearranges its atoms around surfaces into a honeycomb structure of 1 atom thickness. Then the structure expels orphan hydrogen atoms which settle close by. And that creates a battery with positive hydrogens at one end and negative OH ions at another place. This water is silky and kind of dense. Sailors have long noticed that water surrounding ice bergs are silky and dense.

Size & strength of EZ grows when exposed to light, especially IR, thus separating more charge, storing more energy & making the battery bigger. Pure water is best for e-zone. Fluoride, bromine, chlorine & deuterium spoil the battery capacity.

Best way is to get sunlight on the skin, IR penetrates skin 30-40 cm. Natural frequencies from people & pets(warm bodies) also help. IR light is also released by mitochondria when it makes heat. So getting sunlight is the direct method while exposure to cold, eating more food & brown fat are other methods. All this should be directly on your skin.

Fluoride is very harmful as it is a potent dielectric blocker, whether from toothpaste, water or medicine, its always harmful. It also unwinds the triple helix of collagen. Tendon, ligament & cartilage are all collagen which use water to lubricate, so we can easily guess the injuries that fluoride can lead to. When collagen is under tension or compression it releases tiny electric currents (piezo currents) which activate bone regeneration or healing. So guess what a damaged collagen will do to you. Fluoride also forms tiny crystals in soft tissue which acts like sand paper for your joints. It also helps release more calcium into the system, and calcium increases the stress response which is already triggered by EMF, toxins or sleep deprivation. Lastly fluoride displaces iodine, which otherwise help DHA by donating electrons and prevent its oxidation. Bromine, a cousin of fluoride is also bad, it is present in bread products as a supposed 'conditioner'.

Effects of dehydration:

> ➤ Back pain: inter vertebral disks are fluid filled, so drinking lots of water often removes back pain
> ➤ Stomach ulcers:
> ➤ General pain: nerves often interpret high acidity as pain.
> ➤ Asthma
> ➤ Allergies
> ➤ High blood pressure
> ➤ Edema
> ➤ Hormones & insulin issues
> ➤ Headaches: brain cells shrink from lack of water
> ➤ Hard/dry stool or constipation
> ➤ Weaker oxygenation: lungs need to be moist to work better
> ➤ Joint pain/rheumatoid arthritis
> ➤ Digestive problems
> ➤ High cholesterol
> ➤ Disturbed brain function

Magnesium is hydrophilic, it needs water to work, it is used in 50+ enzymatic reactions, so dehydration and magnesium deficiency is a harmful cocktail.

Vitamin D can't be made without water. UV rays are not harmful, it acts harmful when we are dehydrated and lack sulfur (natural sun block), body must be made to develop 'solar callus' through morning exposure. So why so much dehydration? Because of:

➢ nnEMF exposure
➢ inadequate intake
➢ fluoride in water
➢ low moisture in food
➢ weak mitochondria(no ez-water)

how to check health of your mammalian battery:

➢ Sun: what's your solar yield? If its low you are either covered with clothes, or may be exposing in the wrong time. Or your location is not in right place
➢ Water: are you well hydrated? If low you may be around too many people, using too many microwave devices.
➢ DHA: got dha? If low it could be too much blue light, dietary deficiency or poor DHA recycling (again due to blue light)

How to hydrate

➢ Drink more pure water
➢ Avoid fluoride intake, RO water is good
➢ Avoid chlorine intake, keeping overnight in open container drives off chlorine in gas form. But this trick doesn't work on chloramines
➢ Reduce nnEMF exposure, keep distance from phone, switch off at night, drink more water , distance from wifi & switch off at night
➢ Avoid caffein, concentrated sweeteners, salty food
➢ You can try Barbara O'Neil's sea salt "hydration hack"

➢ Spread out the intake, take little water many times instead of all at once
➢ Take moisture rich food, unsweetened tea, unprocessed broth etc
➢ Don't drink water during meals, it dilutes the acids in stomach
➢ Drink deuterium depleted water

Magnetism

Magnetism is very important for health & life. We need unidirectional magnetism to live, as it supports our biology. Without magnetism a person would probably die in about 3 hours. Similar experiment on mice gave similar results. Earth's magnetic field has been decreasing for millions of years. From 300 gauss in dinosaur age to 2.8 gauss 4000 years ago in Babylonian days. Finally 0.5 gauss today with slight variation acc. to location. Its dropping 5-7% every century, this way NASA predicts it will be zero by next 500-800 years. Stronger magnetism produced way larger size & life span for pre historic animals. After it becomes zero, the magnetic field reverses, the poles swap places and a massive die-out happens. This happened 183 times within the last 83 million years. Healthy person can afford to be out of touch from this magnetism for short while(like travelling at 35000 feet), others have psychotic episode, blood clots, strokes etc.

Magnetism energizes the matter within us, regenerates us in sleep, reduces free radical damage & regulate our biorhythms. Just like light, magnetism can also help produce DC electricity by the inverse spin hall effect. Bottom line: magnetism is the mother of all catalysts, more essential than enzymes, more foundational than grounding, more basic to our biology than sunlight.

The brain recharges one organ/tissue in sleep at a time. Brain cells called 'astrocytes' repairs organs by sending them DC voltage. Voltage from astrocytes equals potency of regeneration.

Factors which reduce electrical output from astrocytes:

> Stress
> Heavy metals
> Sleep deficiency
> Foreign frequencies

Because of the above, organs often don't get their fair share of re-energizing 'resonance'.

Primary function of astrocyte cells in brain is to convert chemical energy to electrical energy. It depends on the strength of their mitochondria.

Often electrons cluster more on one side of an atom, and that particular side becomes overweight with polarity and mass. The atom vibrates as one side gets overloaded, just like a washing machine vibrating during spin-drying. In case of tissue this happens at 1-100 times per second. The atom's attractive & repulsive force also increases on that side(briefly) as the charge bunches up. This imbalance of charge & momentum creates a wobble or vibration known as "pre-cession". The rate at which an atom, molecule or organ vibrate is its "natural vibrational frequency". At an atomic level when atoms are together for some time, like in an organ, their valence electrons sync up their wobble and you get a signature rate of vibration which the brain can then use to target that organ for regeneration. Astrocytes thus can target each tissue individually based on need. Resonance is when an atom, molecule or material is exposed to the exact frequency at which it naturally vibrates, whether by sound wave, magnetic force or electrical charge. So resonance is simply adding more of an atom/material's natural frequency to make it vibrate more intensely. Astrocytes sends a pulsed DC current to the entire body along the outer layer of motor and sensory nerves. These pulses produce a magnetic field at right angles to the nerve, the concerned tissues are targeted based on frequency and not on private connections, while non participating atoms are unaffected. Thus only the targeted tissues get the benefit of resonance. But if astrocytes don't communicate with the cells around the body properly, then no resonance occurs and the chance to heal is missed. Finally giving the electrons a push in the wrong direction instead of wrong time not only produce no result but gives opposite result. It slows down the orbital speed and slows down the atom's vibration and decrease its chemical activity, and this is not good for life at all. So non-uniform magnetic fields which are generally found in modern homes & workplaces should be avoided. 'Biofeedback' is the way an astrocyte knows which organ to target for healing.

Overview of healing process:

> Astrocytes convert chemical energy(glucose) into electrical energy. This DC pulse is broadcast around the body, and charged back at night in sleep.

- ➢ Carrier frequencies use macro frequencies to heal, DC flows to organs to resonate and heal them
- ➢ Message frequencies use micro frequencies to communicate, outgoing healing frequencies are coded with instructions for stem cells as to where they are needed & what to become (nerve, blood or bone, etc).
- ➢ Astrocytes collect data based on frequency of organ which is then encoded in large carrier wave, which comes back.

Our sleep cycle is always 90-120 minutes long. During sleep our astrocytes go through a range of frequencies or different organs, once every 90 minutes to 2 hours. By resonating each tissue and adding energy to their electrons, the brain brings back organs to their best shape.

What makes the body go out of resonance and how to counter it.

- ➢ Stress: it's the no 1 reason in all its forms. Whether stressful job, lack of sleep, blue light, past traumas, toxins, foreign frequencies etc, stress depletes the biochemical & biophysical reserves of body. Stress brings heavy metals into the cells.
- ➢ Scar tissue also blocks healing & message frequencies, so avoid surgery as much as you can.
- ➢ nnEMFs: astrocytes turn up their power to overpower man made frequencies but

there is a limit to that also. Using 'magnetico sleep pads' are very helpful.

Exercise strengthens body's electrical circuit. Each time we contract a muscle, the bones, ligaments & muscles emit static electric charges of electrons. As a result astrocytes don't have to work as hard to covert chemical to electrical energy. Bottom line: brain gets more power to heal.

Earth's magnetic field drops during day, increases at night. It also helps us regulate our circadian rhythms. The magnetic field of earth is more in a crater, for instance the famous chikxulub crater in yukatan peninsula, because the crust is thinner and removed compared to rest of the earth. No surprises that New Orleans has a booming sea food culture even though that place is not a place for sea life. Conversely the farther away from earth we go, the weaker the magnetic field and the sicker we will get. Magnetic flux is more at poles than at equator, its 0.3 gauss at equator & 0.6 gauss at poles. Without this design of nature poles would have been devoid of life as all the heat and sun are in the equator. Even in buildings the outer walls & elevator shafts with rebars are more magnetic than middle of rooms. It is observed that employees in common area eat more to make up for this and become fat but executives in offices away from centre of building enjoyed better health.

ATP is needed to remove heavy metals from cell. Non-toxic metals leave the cell around 40-50 millivolts differential at cell wall(58 is normal) and its easier when cells divide. But brain cells don't divide, hence to get rid of these metals, brain needs more charge of 80-110 mv differential.

To get this double voltage mitochondria need to work in full blast with lots of ATP. Factors that crank up ATP:

- ➢ magnetism
- ➢ IR & UV sun exposure
- ➢ Low deuterium level
- ➢ Low heteroplasmy rate
- ➢ A ketogenic diet (periodically)
- ➢ Exercise
- ➢ Cold thermogenesis

The magnetico sleep mat helps this process too. Finally taking DMSA or chlorella throws out those released heavy metals out of body through detox channels.

Oscillation magnetic fields from AC power running through our walls & devices can devastate our health totally. When changing a hemisphere our body electrons have to re-orient to the new magnetic field and it takes 10-12 weeks, till then we feel depleted. Sleeping orientation also matters, sleeping on stomach or on back robs us of energy, best is side sleeping.

DHA, paramagnetism & blood flow

Unlike popular belief, the heart does not pump blood around the body just by mechanical pressure. There are micro capillaries even smaller than the size of RBC. So sheer mechanical force is not enough. Its like a person blowing water through a rubber tube 1mm thick and hundreds of feet in length. The actual reason is electrostatic forces. The inner walls of blood vessel, RBC, plasma all carry different charge at different phases of operation which enhances the blood flow greatly with a little effort from the mechanical force of the beating heart.

6 main function of heart:

- Pulsates the blood flow:
- Vortexes: converts normal flow into vortex
- One way valve: makes the blood flow in correct direction
- Pulse rate: when more oxygen is needed heart beats faster
- Adds propulsion with the blood's paramagnetism
- Structures water molecules in the blood

The heart actually works like a hydraulic ramp pump.

Causes of blood flow breakdown:

> ➢ Excessive friction: to flow freely RBCs have to be surrounded by a cloud of charge particles, called zeta potential. When it drops, friction rises. Healthy zeta potential is -9.3 mV to -15 mV. Grounding, sunlight, etc all previous mentioned factors help maintain healthy zeta potential.
> ➢ Inelastic blood vessels: fluoride breaks down the smooth muscle and elastin fibres of blood vessel rendering them inelastic. Solutions are magnetico sleep pad, DMSA, iodine(minus fluoride).
> ➢ Heart can't pull blood into itself: caused either by frailty of heart's mitochondria or blood has lost paramagnetism by losing zeta potential. Solution is avoiding and getting rid of mitochondrial toxins.
> ➢ Poorly structured blood flow: blood must pulsate, spiral, to avoid losing momentum through capillaries. When blood vessels deteriorate then body makes up with high blood pressure, inflammation, etc. So these are symptoms, not causes, of a distressed bio-physical state (charge, magnetism, light, water, mitochondria).
> ➢ Mis-shaped heart: heart is shaped like a 'chestahedron' (seven-sided). Heart uses sacred geometry (golden ratio 1 : 1.618) to maximise energy entering bloodstream. So its shape is best suited for the job, but its shape changes because of heavy

metals, weak mitochondria, irregular electrical charge etc.

> Impotent e-zone: when its hot outside, body produces more e-zone from IR and adds polarity & propulsion to blood. And when its cold and we lack zeta potential, the body constricts the vessels to keep the blood's momentum up. Bottom line: blood flow is very much the real cause behind diabetes etc. due to low polarity & propulsion.

> Plaque in arteries: narrowing of arteries is caused by body to keep up the velocity of blood. Cholesterol & saturated fats don't cause heart diseases. In fact low cholesterol levels may cause diseases involving heart, brain, nervous system, mood & behaviour, metabolism, infertility & libido.

Paramagnetism:

Oxygen is paramagnetic, which is an important reason which allows it to get exchanged with the cell from blood during respiration. It's more than the standard story of gas exchange we read in high school biology involving partial pressure difference. Magnetism helps oxygen to move through various layers and finally reach the mitochondria.

Diabetes is a disease of weak mitochondria, oxygenation & circulation. It's the same for alzheimer's. Many modern diseases are also caused by 'hormonal disconnection'. Without magnetic field even if hormones are released by master gland, it is not received correctly by worker glands. DHA is the only nutrient found in food that is truly irreplaceable. It can convert light into DC electricity and back. Our body retains it and recycles it through our eyes (short loop) & liver (long loop). Biggest enemies to this are blue light & wireless microwave. Eczema, allergies etc all go away with raised DC electricity by DHA.

DHA is also paramagnetic and is also the healer of leaky gut. When taking DHA supplements it should be made sure that its in sn-2 form, not sn-1 or sn-3 form. Fish oil stored in cold & dark container is good or else DHA is susceptible to temperature & photo oxidation.

Most convenient source of DHA is farmed fish but the best source is seafood. The mercury in seafood is not a problem as long as your 'redox potential' is high & strong.

Future of weight loss lies in bio-physics, not food & exercise

- Light: light has various effects on biology
- Electricity: it has various effects on body. Before year 2000, human could tolerate electric fields. But that is changing fast.
- Mitochondria: new research is finding more about mitochondria but since its basis is energy instead of chemicals, it finds no takers in the pharmaceutical industry.
- Water: light can charge-separate water into e-zone, it's a very new finding
- Non-natural microwave frequencies: people are slowly realizing how 4G, wifi, etc upset our hormone, metabolism, sleep cycle & fertility. 5G will be more sinister. EMFs drain health faster than its believed possible by average jane as they don't like hearing that their favourite company & addictions are killing them.

6 reasons for weight gain:

- Microbiome lacking diversity
- Leakage of light
- Electron deficiency
- Weak mitochondria

> ➢ Leptin resistance
> ➢ High deuterium levels

There is strong connection between obesity and narrowing of microbial species in gut. Diversity in gut bacteria strains has normalising effect on weight. But surprisingly diet or antibiotics are not main reason for narrowing of gut bacteria, its chronic exposure to an altered light spectrum that allows poor diet & antimicrobial threats. Feeding standard American diet (soft drinks, candy, antibiotics) to hunter-gatherer tribe of equator(the 'hadza') didn't change their microbiome at all. Consistent sun exposure protected their microbiome despite a crappy diet.

Leakage of light: every cell emits a very low frequency UV light, but under stress they release more UV light. Obesity is related to this kind of leakage. People with excess fat leak more light.

Electron deficiency or low electron intake: all food ultimately breaks down to electron, proton & photon. So we should focus on quantity (& quality) of electrons, protons & photons that a food offers. Whole & natural foods are best. Processed foods deplete electrons. ATP per calorie is much more of a parameter related to weight loss. Solutions for a wireless world:

> ➢ Eat more good fats (4 times the electrons than carbs)
> ➢ Grounding & sunlight: 33% electron should come from food, 66% from earthing & sunlight (along with drinking

water & getting DHA). So less earth and sun means eating more and being fat.

Weak mitochondria is anther cause of disease and also weight gain. Its not calorie per se that adds weight, its inefficient conversion of calorie to ATP.

Leptin (weight & energy balance hormone)

Endocrine system uses leptin level in blood to regulate appetite so the body weight remains balanced. Leptin is the master controller of essential processes throughout the body. All other processes governing weight gain/loss are subordinate to leptin's direction. We first get leptin in breast milk. Obesity is basically a failure of the leptin system to respond to high leptin levels in blood. Women are more sensitive to leptin & their environment. It's a reason women tend to gain fat easily and has a hard time losing it. Leptin resistance(not insulin resistance) makes you infertile. Major cause of leptin resistance is artificial blue light in the eye and on the skin. Way to guess if you are leptin resistant is to stand naked in front of mirror, too heavy or too thin, both means you are leptin resistant. Low vit-D level is another indicator of leptin resistance. Also hsCRP & reverse T3 tests can tell. But standard thyroid test can mislead you even though thyroid malfunction has a relation with leptin resistance.

Restoring leptin function:

> ➢ DHA: avoid retinal & inflammation damage by taking more DHA by eating more seafood & cold water fish & liver from grass fed animals.

- ➤ Cold exposure: it turns on ancient temperature regulation pathways in all mammals.
- ➤ Brown fat: cold also activates fat-burning pathways that turn white fat into brown fat which produces only heat & no ATP.
- ➤ Reducing all other inflammation: the side benefits of fat-burning pathways are amazing. It also ends all inflammatory conditions like diabetes, heart disease & cancer.

The main way to heal is to allow the brain to see leptin in correct time of the day, and not see it in the wrong time. That's because leptin signalling is linked to day, night, waking & sleep cycles.

Deuterium

It controls survival, growth & maturation in the young and metabolism, aging & disease in the old. It's a common hydrogen atom with one extra neutron in its nucleus. That extra neutron is used to regulate mitochondrial output, biorhythms, etc.

But in excess, deuterium reduces the energy output of mitochondria. Organs which gather more deuterium will be hardest hit by disease as a person ages.

In recent decades, toddlers to adolescents seem to be obese because the ovum gets lots of deuterium even before fertilization, killing 1,00,000 mitochondria. The germ line is damaged and gets passed on to next generation in that defective state. Weak mitochondria is single biggest factor in childhood obesity & disease. In adolescent stage deuterium is responsible for precocious development & early puberty, hence early development of disease also. Basically deuterium makes us age faster.

At the same time deuterium is not always bad, its actually good when present in blood, sperm, egg, wbc, etc. Its bad only when in the wrong place, in wrong amount, wrong time etc.

Effects of high deuterium:

> ➢ Increases inflammation

- ➤ Makes you more sensitive to nnEMFs
- ➤ Affects enzyme function
- ➤ Cancer, MS, osteoporosis, autoimmunity
- ➤ Reduces ATP output, thus increasing risk of autism, brain fog, fibromyalgia, lyme disease
- ➤ Blocks hormone production by disabling cholesterol

Deuterium can change gene expression through epigenetics and is responsible for 90% of diseases. For instance, inefficient conversion of cholesterol into vitamin D and hormones, raises up cholesterol levels while we keep blaming animal fat.

Food rank according to deuterium content:

- ➤ Naturally raised animal product: they have least deuterium, and in fact lower your deuterium level.
- ➤ Vegetables have comparatively higher deuterium levels than animals
- ➤ Fruits have even higher than vegetables, a plant's deuterium is dumped in its fruit
- ➤ GMO has still more than fruits
- ➤ Then comes refined vegetable oils and carbs
- ➤ The highest of all is in 'processed junk food', all the harmful ones mentioned above are together in junk food

Below 20 no person should think about deuterium depletion unless they have chronic health issues, in fact its needed. But in the late 30s or beyond, you might consider reducing the deuterium levels. If deuterium level is to be tested the best is in exhaled air, saliva, blood, urine.

Breath & saliva deuterium levels:

- ➢ Saturated: 'red zone' is over 150 ppm
- ➢ Elevated: 'yellow zone' is 130-150 ppm
- ➢ Desired: 'green zone' is 130 ppm or below
- ➢ Average deuterium level: 137-147 ppm

Ways in which our body expels deuterium:

- ➢ Breathing
- ➢ Urinating
- ➢ Defecating
- ➢ Sweating
- ➢ Metabolism
- ➢ Reproductive cells (sperm, egg, uterine lining)

So it basically means sleep, exercise & reproduction depletes deuterium, the fastest through excretion. Deuterium depletion steps include:

- ➢ Consuming natural oils & fats
- ➢ Eat naturally raised animal products
- ➢ Avoiding non-local fruits (non season fruits)
- ➢ Avoiding grains when not getting UV light
- ➢ Reduce non-local vegetable intake
- ➢ Eat more inland grown plants (not costal)
- ➢ Drink water from higher latitudes (arctic water, etc)
- ➢ Drink natural spring water
- ➢ Drink deuterium-depleted water
- ➢ Get more sun

- ➢ Soak in hot springs
- ➢ Adopt ketogenic diet
- ➢ Have more sex(men)
- ➢ Ovulation & menstruation(women)

You are what you eat

Food takes its order from the physics of life. For a healthy life food probably comes 5th or 6th in importance after real light exposure, magnetism, water quality, man-made EMFs, stress level, grounding & cold exposure. Light, water, magnetism controls how well or poorly food is received and turned into resources by your mitochondria. But only food gets all the attention from so called heath gurus.

Eating some carbs in summertime with some fat is not a threat as:

> - It reduces mitochondrial burn efficiency
> - Makes manageable amount of free radicals
> - Activates autophagy

Farmers love deuterium because it gives them higher agricultural yield.

Leptin reset & cold thermogenesis protocol (by Dr Jack Kreuse)

This protocol is:

> ➤ New & radically different, it focuses on body's impaired energy management system
> ➤ Past failures not a problem
> ➤ Post menopausal women also good candidates for this
> ➤ Willpower not required
> ➤ Any one protocol will also work independently
> ➤ Contraindications: check with your healthcare professional because good changes like better insulin sensitivity or weight loss can affect other treatments in progress.

Warning for darker skin people (equatorial haplotype): don't create infradian mismatches that radically shift heteroplasmy rate. Their mitochondria are already tightly coupled, so cold exposure or fatty food may impact them differently compared to northern European haplotypes.

Visit 'jackkruse.com' for more information on this protocol.

First test if you are leptin resistant.

> - If you are overweight, chances are you are leptin resistant
> - If excessively thin, it means leptin receptors has lost sensitivity to leptin as well
> - Large apetite & carb craving at night are also indicators of the same
> - Elevated 'reverse T3' is sign of leptin resistance in fit people

Know what to eat:

> - Produce: eat in-season vegetable
> - Protein: eat good quality protein, seafood is best, pasture raised organ meat next best, grass fed muscle meat is third best
> - Fats: flavour with fats according to season
> - Oils: avoid nut/seed oils
> - Broth: bone broth of grass fed animals & seafood broth
> - Fermented veggies: eat as much as you can
> - Carbs: if overweight limit carbs to 25gm in breakfast, if average weight then 50gm, if fit then 100gm

Dr Jack Kruse's food pyramid

> - Base of the pyramid (most plentiful) is shellfish like oysters (not crustaceans). For best brain function.
> - Next is crustaceans
> - Followed by fish

- ➢ Then organ meat of pasture raised animals (specially liver)
- ➢ 5th level is grass fed muscle meat
- ➢ Pasture raised eggs
- ➢ At the apex (least plentiful) are nuts & seeds

Foods to avoid

- ➢ All grains
- ➢ All pasteurized & homogenized dairy
- ➢ Nightshade vegetables: if you have chronic inflammation or low vit D

Knowing HOW to eat

- ➢ Eat as soon as possible after waking, preferably within 30 mins of rising. (eggs, meat, poultry, fish)
- ➢ Eat 3 meals a day in beginning, as hunger subsides make it 2
- ➢ Don't snack between meals. It activates the liver frequently & upsets the timing of circadian rhythm to work with leptin. Liver should be trained to make glucose on its own (ketosis)
- ➢ Do not count calories
- ➢ Allow 4-5 hours between dinner & bedtime

Most will notice change in cravings within 4-6 weeks

Supporting actions:

- ➢ Don't exercise before or right after breakfast. Do it after 5pm

- ➢ Trouble sleeping? Do 3-5 mins light exercise before bedtime (pushup, squat). Avoid activities that produce cortisol.
- ➢ Within an hour of sunset, make surroundings as dark as possible, specially reduce exposure to artificial blue light (less insulin). This helps stop cortisol & turn on melatonin and increase detection of leptin by hypothalamus.

Signs that the above protocols are working (increased leptin sensitivity)

- ➢ Rapid weight loss for men
- ➢ Women will notice mood changes (calmer, centered), improved sleep(huge clue), initial weight change minimal but clothes could fit differently.
- ➢ Change in sweating patterns (for both genders)
- ➢ Better recovery from exercise
- ➢ Higher energy level
- ➢ Diminished hunger & cravings
- ➢ Feeling refreshed after sleep
- ➢ Hair, nails, skin look healthier
- ➢ Carb cravings subside
- ➢ You'll feel warmer but body temperature will go down
- ➢ Thoughts, mood, personality normalize
- ➢ Mental acuity, insight, intuition & libido improve

Iodine normalizes thyroid function, helps fat burning pathway & weight.

Most women & some men nowadays have depressed thyroid function which makes them gain weight and hard to lose it. Other signs are thin hair, brittle nails, cold extremities, dry skin & chronic fatigue. Reason for such hypothyroidism are:

  ➢ Fluoride accumulation in thyroid
  ➢ Leptin resistance
  ➢ Autoimmunity to your thyroid
  ➢ Circadian disruption
  ➢ nnEMF exposure
  ➢ radioactive isotopes

Iodine raises thyroid hormone levels to an optimal range, it also turns on uncoupling proteins (fat burning help). Iodine is of great importance, never ignore it.

Cold thermogenesis protocol:

You can start by dunking your face in cold water till you can hold your breath. It sends signal that you are in cold environment. 10-12 degree Celsius is enough, no need to get a frost bite. In fact any temperature below 36 degree Celsius makes mitochondria release more heat. After you are habituated with face dunks, soak full body in a tub of cold water as much as you can bear as many times per week. Build up to 15, 30 mins and higher. The colder the water you can tolerate the better.

Warning: don't use cold thermogenesis when healing from a sports type injury, as it will oppose inflammation which is actually needed for healing.

How friendly frequencies support our biology

Many forms of electromagnetism occurs naturally on earth & universe which are good for us. Natural vibration teaches brain & nervous system, the vibration rate at which they work best. The best example of this is "schumann resonance". Vibrating at 7.83 cycles per second, it is said to originate from energy waves such as lightning strikes & cosmic rays circumnavigating the globe.

It's the quintessential friendly frequency. 7.83 Hz is our body's neutral zero point. It's the baseline calibration frequency between normal (9-12Hz) during daytime and 8 to under 1 Hz of nighttime. Two other frequencies that support human biology are IR & UV. Sunlight is far more than it appears to be. It consists of 7 colours and the composition of the colours change over the course of the day, and over the seasons as the light penetrate the atmosphere from different angles. Each colour control different aspects of biology through our eyes and skin with the help of suprachiasmatic nucleus (SCN).

Natural light is whole food, man-made light is junk food. Natural sunlight has various co-factors which gives you healthy, balanced effect. But in order to be energy efficient, artificial light is like mostly one colour, specially blue, no purple or red frequencies. Its like junk food, full of sugar (stimulation) but low in fiber (moderation). Sun is accused of giving us cancer, wrinkle & eye problems but at least 8 large scale meta-studies have shown that all-cause mortality goes down the more sun you get. But the controversy is because everyone can't capture and use sunlight. Yes its possible to get problem to skin & eyes from too much sun ONLY if you don't have good redox potential to repair it. Like exercise, you have to build up to higher intensities. If sun hurts your eyes, you squint & blink, that means you are solar deficient, you need more IR & UV. Blinking is designed to moisten cornea and make you absorb even more UV light. Finally its not just the quantity of sunlight but how well your body & mitochondria can incorporate that light.

Each frequency of light penetrates the tissue to different depths:

> ➢ Infrared: it penetrates the deepest (10-30 cm). It can reach even the internal organs and charge up the water in the cell and mitochondria with electric potential.
> ➢ Blue light: penetrates 3-6 cm which is bad news for the thyroid which sits a centimetre below the skin. Thyroid release hormone non stop and all kinds of problems surface.
> ➢ Ultraviolet: its biofriendly but too much is problematic. Dark skin nature's first step to limit too much UV intake. Dead skin cell on surface of skin is another trick of natural sun block. But when you need more UV, body release more nitric oxide which brings more light capturing blood

to the skin surface as UV penetrates few millimetres.

Effect of light on biology is non-linear, means it doesn't follow the 'effect proportional to input' rule. Even modest exposure to certain frequencies can produce big effects.

> ➢ Your biochemicals close for the day when UV-A shows up in late morning
> ➢ You need 1-3 mins of blue light from morning sun to set your internal clock for the day (if consistent)
> ➢ Some frequencies control almost 1,00,000 biochemicals
> ➢ Many ailments like type-2 diabetes get worse after cataract operation when UV light cant get through artificial lens implants

Our bodies incorporate light in many ways through numerous biochemical reactions.

How light becomes energy, matter & physiologic function:

> ➢ Chromophores: for instance water is a red light chromophore, it absorbs all frequencies of red and circulates the union around the body
> ➢ Photoreceptors: they are not just to convert light into electrical signal, they are simply receptors of light in the eye, skin, fat & blood vessels which help control daily & seasonal processes.

Opsins are a special type of receptors, its types are:

> ➢ Melanopsin: it's the blue light detector in eyes, skin, fat & blood vessels.
> ➢ Neuropsin: it's the UV-A detector in eye & skin
> ➢ Rhodopsin: found in rod cells absorbs mainly green & blue light
> ➢ Photopsins: also called cone-opsins are found in cone cells, help us see colour

Porphyrins: they are present in haemoglobin and help the blood to carry light around the body, same role is also played by water as chromophore.

Fluorophores: its an organic compound which can absorb light at one frequency and emit it at a different wavelength, mostly in UV range. Dentin & tooth enamel are also fluorophore protein.

Important biochemicals are first made in the eye, hence getting full spectrum sunlight on your eyes & skin is the 2nd best way to improve sleep quality (after magnetico sleep pad).

Blue light: it basically has a stimulating effect on our biology, lighter the blue, more stimulation it is. But now biorhythms are messed up by getting exposed to too much blue from technology and that too all day long.

Infrared light: it is the antidote to the stimulatory effects of blue, designed by nature for balance. IR forms e-zone which uses its electricity to heal.

Red light has the superpower of elevating our energy levels, healing capacity, resistance to aging. It makes more ATP without electron from food, brown fat or grounding. Its almost like a substitute for food to some extent. Red light bio-hacks:

> Infrared lamps: simply shine an infrared lamp in your room or workspace to offset the effects of blue. It also fills the gaps when your ac powered light strobes at 50hz per second.
> Red light therapy: many devices use visible or invisible red light to give therapeutic benefits. Joovv red light device is a good one to try.
> Gold foil: in case you have home sauna, you can increase your infrared exposure by lining its walls with real gold foil (not gold coloured foil). Real gold is great infrared reflector.

UV light:

It's the most underappreciated & vilified light in modern world, but human biology evolved to use it. Four ways to feel the effects of UV:

> UV gives you a natural high by making a biochemical called POMC.
> UV naturally lowers the blood pressure by dilating blood vessels with nitric oxide
> UV calms the sympathetic stress response from paraventricular nucleus
> UV is a natural calcium channel blocker, which reduces stress response.

Nature wouldn't have blessed us with UV if it was harmful. Sunglass, contact lens & glass blocks UV light. Using them makes our pupil dilate more than normal and allows light more than we should tolerate. Normal window glass blocks 75% UV-A and 100% UV-B. Car windshield are specially treated to block UV-A. Surprisingly just living indoors automatically makes you blue light toxic. Its simply quantum malnutrition to mindlessly block sun.

Sun exposure & sun damage is not the same. Exposure can make the skin look uneven or aged in the short term but it's not damage as the uneducated observer might think, its actually use & conditioning. Mortality from diseases like skin cancer goes down with sun exposure. Fix your relation with light and skin will look better long term:

> Get morning sun on eye & skin
> Drink good quality water
> Avoid blue light at night
> Avoid nnEMFs
> Eat deuterium depleting foods
> Get more sulphur in diet
> Do everything to tune up your mitochondria

How to harvest UV light:

UV-A reaches 0.3mm skin deep, UV-B reaches 0.1mm deep, UV-C reaches 0.05mm deep. So the main step to do is getting the blood to the surface of the skin. UV on skin releases nitric oxide which dilates blood vessels. RBC containing porphyrins reach there to pick up the UV and deliver it to cells.

People living at high latitudes have difficulty harvesting UV because at the angle at which sun enters the atmosphere specially in darker months. Some workarounds:

- ➢ Higher elevations get more UV, so skiing on mountains in winter is a good strategy to make up.
- ➢ Aluminium foil is good reflector of UV. (old face-tan reflectors)
- ➢ Even if its cloudy, don't miss sun exposure as the little UV that makes through the clouds means a lot. Remember light works in "non-linear" fashion.

Seven tips for UV harvesting as nature intended:

- ➢ Build your solar callus: IR-A prepares the skin to receive UV later in the day without sunburn. Or an IR-A lamp can help in its place though not as effective. Carbs also has a similar effect by thickening the skin but depending solely on carbs for this effect is not recommended for obvious reasons.
- ➢ Adequate hydration: you cant make vitamin D in dehydrated state. Causes of dehydration include nnEMFs, coffee, tea, poor mitochondrial function, etc
- ➢ Sulphur: it helps us capture good sunlight while reflecting the bad frequencies
- ➢ Avoid polyunsaturated omega-6 fatty acid (linoleic acid): vegetable oil is bad for you including corn, safflower,

sunflower, cottonseed, soyabean, canola, etc
➢ Natural sunblock: dead cells on the skin surface unwind their DNA, which act as natural protection against overexposure. So exfoliating may make you look younger short term, but older long term.
➢ Avoid chemical sunblock: it blocks the UV you need badly. Both sunscreen & make-up are bad
➢ Avoid UV blocking materials: even see through material alters the full spectrum of the sunlight
➢ More electrons: the more you can acquire and retain electrons the better you are able to capture & use sunlight. Light can only interact with electrons

Sunlight on our private parts is very important. Lack of it contributes to reproductive disfunction like erectile dysfunction, prostate problems, lack of libido & infertility in both sexes. If privacy allows you then make sure to expose those areas to sunlight often or else you may try UV permeable bathing suits. Kiniki & cooltan are two good brands producing such suits.

Winter & fall sunbathing: northerners face challenge in getting enough sun, as it's a problem to go shirtless or pantless in such cold to get the meagre sun that comes. One solution is to place a heating pad below you which stays warm for around 15-20 minutes and then exposing your skin and eyes to full spectrum sunlight.

To conclude, we need light just as much as plants do. Our real solution lies in the quality of our light, water, magnetism & mitochondria.

How man made EM-frequencies hurt us

Energetically earth used to be a nice, quiet place to live. So EM frequencies that existed thousands of years ago is beneficial & tolerable to us. However we are not built to tolerate frequencies & intensities that were not present in ancient earth. Its stressful at best but harmful or even deadly over time. At present, we are literally swimming in a sea of invisible, unhealthy, non-native EM radiations that clashes with the schumann resonance and overpowers it.

Smart meters which wirelessly beam your electricity usage readings to the company, use microwave frequencies, imagine what a neighbourhood full of these machines are causing. Worse than this are our phones which are closer to us all day long, they vibrate our brain with alien frequency when we hold them against our heads. It makes our brain even more sensitive to these frequencies apart from other complications like tumors etc. Its very hard to trace back modern day health problems back to these factors.

The power grid is very toxic (AC power)

Stray voltage around the home wiring & electric fields around devices are very harmful to health. We never had to worry much about it before the wifi & 4g era as we had extra healing capacity to spare &

could tolerate a fair amount of these stressors. AC power (6ohz) of north America messes mitochondria and results in obesity, neuro degeneration & cancer. AC power (5ohz) of Europe causes more electro-hypersensitivity to nnEMFs. Even low voltage DC power devices are also problematic when used close to the body.

AC upsets biological systems far more than DC as it oscillates faster than natural frequencies of the body that recharge & regenerate the cells. The future holds the promise of AI, making self-driving cars & smart cities a reality, raising the roof on the saturation of our airwaves. It will deplete whatever regeneration ability we have left.

Dirty electricity is the most harmful, also called electromagnetic interference (EMI) or high-frequency voltage transients (HFVT), they are caused by:

- ➢ Irregularities in electricity generation in power plants
- ➢ Appliances drawing power from shared lines (power supplies)
- ➢ Airbourne nnEMFs captured on power lines & brought to home

These disturbances exaggerate wear & tear on your device as well as your mitochondria.

Common sources of dirty electricity:

- ➢ Compact florescent light bulbs
- ➢ Smart meters
- ➢ Dimmer switches on LED lights (create abrupt on/off transitions)

- ➢ Microwave, fridge, plasma TV, computer power supply
- ➢ Variable speed HVAC, well & swimming pool pumps
- ➢ Cell towers
- ➢ Wiring errors
- ➢ Solar or wind power
- ➢ Electric car battery charger
- ➢ Even trees brushing up against power line

Dirty electricity remedies:

- ➢ A meter can be used to test the acuity of domestic dirty electricity (< $200)
- ➢ Specialist can be hired for more thorough analysis
- ➢ Simple test is to turn off circuit breakers at night and see if health improves

Once risk level is assessed, installing filters in electrical outlets or at breaker panels can help.

For best result hire a nnEMF remediation specialist as there can be intricacies involved. You can also install a whole-home filter at your breaker box rather than individual filters around the house.

AC power shakes our cells more than the brain's regenerative frequencies of 12hz to under 1hz. It overpowers the body's own healing messages. Countries with 50hz electricity closely competes with mitochondria's optimal fat & protein burning frequency of 100hz. It results in more free radicals, less ATP, lower healing capacity.

The ETC (electron transport chain) burns fat best when cytochromes vibrate at 100hz. That means 50hz power (2nd harmonic of 100hz) messes mitochondria's ability to burn fat & protein by screwing up ETC.

60hz power makes Americans over indulge in carbs as 60hz interferes less with cytochrome (I) and ETC as it's the 5th harmonic of 100hz (60 * 5 = 300). Europeans due to their 50hz develop more electro-hypersensitivity while Americans with their 60hz tend to get heavier.

Ground current is the electricity beneath our feet, it is caused by improper wiring in our houses. It makes it unsafe for us to ground in populated areas. It results in foot sores, low milk production in cows.

Blue light:

Artificial blue light ruins our circadian rhythm more than any toxin known to man. It doesn't contain the red & purple parts present in natural sunlight which counteracts the harmful effects of blue. Man made blue light is so harmful because:

> - Screens and bulbs emit a blue which is 3 or 4 times colour intensity of original
> - We get it way too often in a day
> - We are exposed to it way too long
> - We get it at the wrong times of the day
> - Its usually alone without any counter-balancing frequencies (red-purple)

Incandescent bulbs of olden days were almost same as natural sunlight. Unfortunately now we are ruled by LEDs. Blue light causes:

- ➢ Adrenal fatigue
- ➢ Brain & behaviour problems (attention deficit disorder)
- ➢ Metabolic disfunction (diabetes, obesity)
- ➢ Fertility problems
- ➢ Addictions (social media, chemicals & p*rn)

Toxicity of blue light causes:

- ➢ Increased heteroplasmy rate: lowers mitochondrial efficiency
- ➢ Dehydrates you: sluggish mitochondria makes less water, hence less e-zone, slower detoxification, protein malformation
- ➢ Activates the stress response: upsets hormonal system, contributes to type-2 diabetes
- ➢ Wrecks DHA function in the eye/brain: weak mitochondria make small magnetic field, and DHA is moved around in blood by magnetism
- ➢ Creates brain fog & over-spends dopamine: you become slave to stimulation in your environment, in other words ADD
- ➢ Disturbs melatonin & sleep: by melanopsin-vitamin A degradation
- ➢ Impairs thyroid function: blue light penetrates 3-6cm of skin, so long exposures wreck mitochondria function in thyroid

- ➢ Upsets the testosterone production/ovulatory cycles: contributes to sexual disfunction, infertility
- ➢ Increases reactive oxygen species: causes more free radicals, inflammation, aging
- ➢ Exaggerates metabolic problems: raises glucose levels, suppresses insulin
- ➢ Promote vitamin A deficiency & obesity: turns retinol toxic (retinal)

In humans photoreceptors are loosely bound to retinol (vitamin A), blue light destroys this loose covalent bond and vitamin A becomes toxic, an aldehyde called 'retinal' which is a rogue version of retinol (vit A). It blows other molecules to bits, and running amok in the body destroys all photoreceptors. Macular degeneration & cataracts are increasing day by day.

Retinal attacks melanopsin, melatonin, respiratory proteins & metabolism. So blue light interferes with sleep, mitochondrial vitality, and photoreceptor repair via melatonin.

So the subversive reason for people's weakness & sickness is:

- ➢ Too much blue light crashing the melanopsin system
- ➢ Impaired melanopsin crippling the CRP function
- ➢ Disabled CRP then wiping out mitochondrial population & productivity

Blue light is also the culprit that causes myopia (short-sightedness). Since blue light bends more than other colours in a denser medium (ex: prism/eye), our eyes have to force their point of focus further back to compensate for that. After prolonged torture in this way, myopia is caused in addition to genetic factors off course. Myopia can be considered as an 'early warning sign' of mitochondrial distress.

Blue light is the cause of insulin resistance too, as retinal damages respiratory proteins. Still medical world is busy with treating symptoms instead of fixing the actual cause. As of 2020-2021, artificial blue light is the most destructive toxin to modern man, but it will soon be dethroned from that position by 5G, as it ramps up in cities around the world.

Non-native EMFs:

It is argued that nnEMFs are not harmful as they are not ionising, that means they cant knock electrons off atoms like the radioactive radiations do. But its not fully true, it just does the damage in other ways. They raise intra-cellular calcium which causes electron loss through oxidative chemical exchange, instead of displacing electrons through bombardment as in ionising radiations.

Effects of nnEMFs as per Dr Martin Pall's analysis:

- ➢ Lowered fertility (18 reviews)
- ➢ Neurological/psychiatric effects (25 reviews)
- ➢ 3 types of DNA damage (21 reviews)
- ➢ Compromised apoptosis (13 reviews)
- ➢ Oxidative stress/free radical damage (19 reviews)

- ➢ Endocrine/hormonal effects (12 reviews)
- ➢ Excessive intra-cellular calcium (15 reviews)
- ➢ Cancer (35 reviews)

Non ionizing EMFs can be even more damaging than ionizing ones because:

- ➢ Microwave EMFs over-activate voltage-gated calcium channels, allowing more than a million calcium ions ($Ca2+$) to flow into the cell per second.
- ➢ Calcium makes more nitric acid & superoxide radicals
- ➢ These super radicals called peroxynitrite are highly reactive oxidant which breaks down cell wall & proteins

Guess what ! world governments seem to know that nnEMFs are harmful:

- ➢ China: pregnant women are required by law to wear EMF shielding belly bands
- ➢ Israel: cell phones must carry the warning saying that the device causes cancer
- ➢ France: wifi was banned in nursery schools in 2014
- ➢ Russia: Putin said that no need to have war with America, they are committing collective suicide, we just have to wait until they are all in hospital
- ➢ World health organization: in 2011 microwave was declared as a class 2B possible human carcinogen (increased risk of brain cancer)

In addition the countries which have set their radio frequency exposure safety limit 100 to 10,000 times lower than the US are: Italy, Switzerland, France, Austria, Luxembourg, Bulgaria, Poland, Hungary, Israel, Russia & China.

Some symptoms of nnEMF exposure:

➤ Headaches
➤ Ringing in ears
➤ Brain fog
➤ Insomnia
➤ General fatigue
➤ Irritability/stress

Health outcomes:

➤ Sleep problems
➤ Infertility, sexual disfunction
➤ Leaky gut, food sensitivities
➤ Diabetes, obesity
➤ Alzheimer's, parkinson's, dementia,
➤ DNA damage, cancer

Sources of EM pollution:

➤ Cell phones
➤ Smart meters (electricity & gas)
➤ Wifi
➤ "smart" appliances (internet of things)
➤ Home cordless phones, use 2.4 Ghz (most harmful frequency for reproductive system)
➤ Alarm systems
➤ Baby monitors
➤ Police & fire systems
➤ Fluorescent & LED bulbs

- ➢ Air traffic radars
- ➢ Cars (modern cars come with installed wireless system)

nnEMF & dehydration corrupts our biology. Dehydration worsens EMF symptoms because:

- ➢ You cant assimilate as much energy from light (as e-zone water)
- ➢ Magnesium doesn't work very well in enzymatic reactions
- ➢ Skin can't turn cholesterol into vitamin D
- ➢ Weakened mitochondria cant produce "metabolic water"

In case you mainly focussed on remaining healthy then remember these 4 points:

- ➢ Harvesting energy from light
- ➢ Maximising mitochondrial function
- ➢ Improving enzyme function
- ➢ Having all the vitamin D your body needs

Having no water basically means losing battery capacity.

The effect of stress:

nnEMF (spl blue light) causes a stress response. nnEMFs put your nervous system into a prolonged sympathetic state (opposed to rest & digest which is parasympathetic). This stress response during waking hours of the day is perfectly fine and even needed to be alert. But having this response all the time is like putting the body in flight or fight mechanism non-stop. This depletes you of biochemicals which otherwise help in higher functions like concentration & creativity. Blue light in particular tells the body its noon all the time, and whole day the body is inundated with stress chemicals to keep you alert. This wears on the adrenals, the brain & heart like racing a car designed for the streets. Other stressors are also contributing non-stop:

> ➢ Mental/emotional stress
> ➢ Modern chemical & environmental stress: bisphenol-A, artificial lights, irregular sleep patterns, etc
> ➢ Past & future stress: childhood traumas, rape, war related, etc Obsessively worrying about future is also harmful

All stressors basically have a cumulative effect on the adrenals and the body. nnEMFs are also causing forest fires by pushing trees to their limits. So basically every time you are buying a 5G or IOT device, you empower the telecom companies to destroy our ecosystem by legally obligating them to build more networks.

Some other effects of stress:

> ➢ Heavy metals: stress leads to heavy metal buildup in cells.
> ➢ Digestion: high cortisol shuts down stomach acid production
> ➢ Glucose & insulin resistance: stress & cortisol also flood the body with glucose
> ➢ Immune system: cortisol shuts down the immune system
> ➢ Blood flow: stress directs blood flow away from organs to peripheral organs

> ➤ Sleep & repair: cortisol & adrenalin inhibit sleep & healing

How body responds to stress:

> ➤ Biophoton loss: cells normally release low UV light but under stress they release biophotons faster, like a leaking gas tank.
> ➤ Electron deficiency: nnEMFs like blue light also cause electron loss, so less electrons are available for healing & regeneration.

nnEMFs ruin sleep quality & deplete magnesium. Calcium tenses muscles and magnesium relaxes them. But all day long EMF exposure makes the muscles contract and depletes the magnesium which is trying to relax them.

Simple test to find if adrenals are over stressed: shine a penlight in your eye in a dark room. If the pupil starts to pulsate then the adrenals are fatigued. Solution: cut blue light at night, shield sleeping & working spaces from nnEMFs, enjoy full spectrum sun on eyes & skin.

Frequency of EMF determines type of free radical produced: said simply it means that specific wavelength of microwave radiation produces a different kind of mitochondrial poison and therefore a different kind of illness. We can just wait & see what 5G does in future according to different land and frequency range. Women are more vulnerable to EMFs than men, children more than women and babies in womb the most.

Prof. Neelima Kumar of Punjab University showed how cell towers are destroying the metabolism of bees, and they are going extinct.

More nnEMF concerns:

> It opens the blood-brain barrier & gut barrier: perforating the blood brain barrier is especially bad for people with autism, ADD & children
> Microbes excrete biotoxins under threat:
> It turns probiotic microorganisms into aggressive pathogens:
> Nighttime exposure is much worse than daytime:

Heavy metals scatter nnEMF transmissions: mercury and aluminium increase the injury caused by nnEMFs as they break up the signals and make them bounce around inside the body. The EMF goes haywire inside the cells, compounding the damage. Its one of the reason a vaccine is bad for you as the aluminium-based adjuvants deflect biophotons thus interfering with body's own internal communication.

Metals also act as antennas, and some common sources are:

> Tattoos: coloured ink contains metals, for instance red is made up of lots of iron which inhibit skin from assimilating sunlight
> Mercury amalgam fillings & dental fixtures
> Orthopedic hardware

> ➢ Metal-frame glasses
> ➢ Underwire bras
> ➢ Metal belt buckles & metal jewellery
> ➢ Heavy metals: toxic metals respond to microwave and radio frequencies

5th generation wireless (5G)

5G is set to become the biggest destructive force about to be unleashed on terrestrial biology. People will come down with serious unexplained illnesses, without any history or traditional risk factors. Conditions to expect:

> ➢ Cognitive decline
> ➢ Autoimmune disorders
> ➢ Metabolic syndrome
> ➢ Cancer
> ➢ Suicide
> ➢ Psychosis
> ➢ Heart attack/stroke
> ➢ Allergies

All these will become frighteningly common.

But the question arises that why is suddenly 5G so dangerous, why not 4G, 3G, 2G etc. That's because of the nature of the 5G signal, unlike previous ones 5G runs of a lower transmission power & higher density of signal, thus creating a blanket of millimetre waves surrounding us every minute. What's worse, 5G signal waveform will be "micro shaped" meaning it will have smaller waveforms embedded on larger waves, just like how dirty electricity rides on 60hz power. Damage will be proportional to:

- ➢ No. of transceiver nodes one is exposed to
- ➢ The proximity of the signal
- ➢ Multitude of directions from which they hit us
- ➢ Range of frequencies involved
- ➢ The damage potential of micro structuring the waveform
- ➢ Amount of time one is exposed

Previous technologies were designed to connect you to one tower at a time, but in 5G data packets are broken up and routed through multiple towers. It will cause more injury than single tower technology thus far. What's worse, 4G transmitters will now be embedded in 5G cell nodes (every 500 feet). 4G travels farther than 5G and penetrates deeper into human flesh. So then we will get the worst of both worlds, virulence of 4G & the proximity of 5G.

5G was specifically designed to carry the signals of internet of things (IoT) devices. So in future, outdoor cell phone signals are not the only problem, it will also bombard your body with two-way microwave from cell phones, laptops, tablets, TVs, refrigerators, washing machines, dish washers, microwave ovens, toasters, light bulbs, doorbells, baby monitors, surveillance cameras, speakers & everything else corporate & government can possibly put on a network. And that's just one network out of dozen other harmful network. We are about to live in a microwave oven in future, well almost !

5G is designed for surveillance and centralized control. Its not about connection speed, safety or security because optical fibre can do all that faster, safer and hacker-proof way. 5G is not even about making life easier, better connected, etc. Its actually about spying on people and controlling every aspect of their life, that's how it was conceived and designed from the ground up. Sceptics won't believe but that is why masters behind telecom companies pushing 5G as hard as they can. Its military technology designed to know everything about you, what you're buying, who you talking to, where you are travelling, what you're saying, etc, and with the help of AI, probably what you are likely to think & do next will be predicted as well. Its like wall-to-wall surveillance & control with a few benefits thrown in so that the mindless masses accept it & agree on their own enslavement and servitude (paid by themselves).

But if we have done nothing wrong, should we still fear? Well how would it be if our bank accounts are docked for electricity & water in unapproved ways? You cannot question or else penalties will be automatic and irreversible. What if you are slapped with civil disobedience penalties? What if you are thrown in jail for objecting to fluoridation of water, mandatory vaccination, GMOs, taxes, govt. policies, critical race theory, forced drugging of your kids with 'Ritalin' to attend public schools. What if your kids are taken away from you for teaching them traditional values or the religion of your choice? How about your bank accounts being shut off or retirement accounts deleted? All because you spoke against injustice? Well 5G & IoT make all of these very easy!

For example: China has rolled out a social scoring system for a few years now & Australia is also about to roll out one. China is implementing a state sponsored surveillance & enforcement with their social credit scoring system where you could be fined electronically. Suppose if you write article criticizing the Chinese government, you could lose social credit points. Suppose you protest or break the law, you could be denied a bank loan, a job, a travel permit, a credit card, social services or even health care(if you have very low social score). So that's what 5G really hold for all of us, as some wise person defined it as follows: "SMART = surveillance marketed as revolutionary technology".

Freakish effects of 5G:

> Jump condition: power density of 5G is so great that it can accumulate on conductive materials and 'jump' to other materials. This can lead to release of static electricity, almost like electrocution. For instance it can accumulate on street lights and jump to hand rails & manhole covers. It can accumulate on home electrical wiring and jump to water pipes, gas lines, metal studs, electric wiring and create a nasty field of dirty electricity. (in your bedroom if you're that unlucky)

> Unexplained fires: 5G can cause lesser solar projections to cause fires as it brings down the threshold of our power grids to withstand coronal mass ejections. Many believe this is the cause of Santa Rosa fires of 2017 which happened just after 5G network was activated in that area.

Some buildings were levelled as if hit by an atom bomb. Only trees were safe, and recovered quickly even after being singed.

Instant signs of 5G damages to look out for:

- ➢ Water main breaks
- ➢ Changes in earthquake activity
- ➢ Underground fires
- ➢ Fires at gas station due to 5G phones

Now telecom companies are about to beam 5G from satellites down on us. By 2021 hundreds of such satellites had already gone up. May be metal roofing and building from ground up with EMF blocking materials is the only way forward.

If you are a big city dweller, you already have 5G. If you live near a major airport or military installation, you already are swimming in a 5G environment. What's worse, telecom companies know very well the damage their products are doing but they hide data & confuse people. One study found that the best frequency to cause infertility is 2.4 gigahertz, and that's the exact frequency the FCC chose to let companies use without license or active oversight. Hence its used in cordless phones, baby monitors, wifi, Bluetooth, microwave ovens, car alarms, wireless microphones, among others. What a coincidence that lines up with our plummeting fertility rate. The telecom industry has already taken steps to decrease their liability by law, in case the population faces death or health issues because of cell towers. Cell towers cant be stopped by a law that protects them.

Telecom leaders keep their own children away from nnEMFs. Apple has a feature which turns off the wifi in their iphones & ipads when they are idle but this feature is not advertised. That means they also know and are taking steps to reduce the harm caused. But saying so means they admit knowing it, so they keep shut about it. Steve jobs never let his own children use the products his own company was producing. So was his death from pancreatic cancer karma, or coincidence?

Bill Gates also did not allow his children to use wireless devices, it seems he knows it as well and so does the whole industry. An insurance company called 'Lloyd's of London' which is notorious for insuring things other companies won't touch, refused to insure tech companies against health claims caused by 5G. Now that speaks a lot !

With 5G, we are moving into uncharted territory. There is no research to say its safe. 5G could be so blatantly bad that telecom companies might finally have to admit its dangers and are forced to change it to make it safer for people.

Non native EMF remedies

Basically we have to become our own health boss as the companies are determined to not admit to the adverse effects until its evident enough and the backlash becomes too strong to ignore. You will have to:

- ➢ Know enough so that you are not easily fooled
- ➢ Spend some money on health and wellness from time to time
- ➢ Try some bio-hacks to find out what's best for you
- ➢ Adopt lifestyle changes that result in good outcomes
- ➢ You will have to learn a little about light, water, magnetism & mitochondria

Its almost a decade that we are in collective denial but people are waking up slowly, though not enough still. Exquisite health depends on two things mainly:

- ➢ Getting your exposures right (light, water, magnetism)
- ➢ Ridding your living spaces of nnEMFs

These are the two most powerful approach to reversing illness & attaining wellness beyond appearance. Starting from now you have to increase the 'native' EMF exposures in your life while purge the unnatural frequencies from your routine at every opportunity.

Get as much real sunlight as possible on your eyes & skin:

> See sunrise as often as you can, also sunset too if you can. This is most important to boost your circadian & biophysical health.
> Get as naked as possible when outside in the sun, let the sun hit the skin. Use UV permeable outfits if you want to be more presentable in public
> During sun exposure, avoid sunglasses, eyeglasses, contact lens, window glass as they all block UV and a part of IR. UV & sunlight also improves eyesight
> For every hour of indoor blue light exposure during the day, take a 5 minutes sun break
> Don't use sunscreen, instead acclimate yourself to more sun without burning by hybrid tanning as mentioned in earlier chapter

Reduce your bad-light exposure:

> If turning off blue light isn't possible, swap it out or avoid it, then block it through the eyes, and on skin
> A company called 'bluetec' makes clear glasses with 50% blue blocking power. You can also block 100% by putting an amber coloured tint like BPI (brain power incorporated brand) to any lens.

Or readymade blue blocking goggles are also available.

- ➢ Modern gadgets have settings or apps that shift the screen colour away from blue towards red. But blue blocking glasses are better.
- ➢ The more indoor blue light you face, the more its important to cover your skin with clothing. In particular, cover the throat area, when using smartphones, LED tv, laptops, because blue light penetrates into the thyroid. So button your collar till the top, use a scarf or start using turtle necks.
- ➢ For women, nighttime is the time you can put lots of makeup in order to shield from blue light. (how safe the make up chemicals are, is a different topic)

Choosing the healthiest light bulbs:

- ➢ Remember like a mantra, real sunlight is good for you & artificial light after dark is bad for you
- ➢ Best is fire, so candle or a lamp after sunset is best. Next comes incandescent bulbs of the past. After that comes halogen bulbs and candlelight-style OLED bulbs. Towards the worse comes warm LED, cool LED & fluorescent bulbs, with warm LED being slightly better and fluorescent being the worst.

Its possible to save electricity with energy saving bulbs but you will have to spend more on medical bills on the long run. That's called being 'penny-wise' and 'pound-foolish'. LED & fluorescent bulbs are cheaper but it makes you sicker, dumber & more controllable.

Light prescriptions:

> ➢ Use candle light, patio fire-pit, oil lamps as your light source at night.
> ➢ If that's too unrealistic for you, shift to incandescent bulbs to places where you spend much time, and LED in places where health risk is none. (security light, attic light)

Strategies to mitigate wireless nnEMFs

It starts with EMF awareness, learn when & where you are exposed to it, what dangers they present you, and how to avoid their influence. For instance, instead of streaming music or videos, download them first when the device is away and play it later from internal memory. Simple strategies like this can cut down EMF exposure by a factor of 10 to 100 or more. Simple assessments like how your brain feels by cordless phone use, specially on the side you rest the phone. Is it warm, tingly? then beware.

General guidelines to reduce nnEMF exposure:

> ➢ Increase distance (inverse square law): distance is your friend when it comes to nnEMFs. Inverse law states that nnEMF exposure goes down in proportion to square of distance. That means if you double the distance from source, your exposure is not just halved but quartered.

- ➢ Decrease exposure time: its not easy because blue light & social media are addictive by nature. Find the off buttons and give the real world a try, its hard but natural light gives you the pleasure chemicals so you depend less on technology.
- ➢ Population density: biggest exposure concern how many people live & work around you. This is one issue where you have no solution other than moving to a less populated area.
- ➢ Night exposure is much worse than daytime: activating the stress response during night with microwaves messes the hormones, metabolism & regeneration more than during the day. So mitigate night exposure first, day exposure second. Shield at least the bedroom from nnEMFs.
- ➢ DHA, oxygen & water: more the blue light & nnEMF exposure, more DHA, oxygen & water you need to offset their damages.

Tips to reduce nnEMF exposure:

- ➢ Filter dirty electricity out of your living spaces
- ➢ Reduce exposure to electricity: move bed away from walls with electric wires running through them, turn off devices when not in use
- ➢ Choose devices that use less power, battery power is preferable. DC current is better

> Check for bipolar magnetic fields in your most frequented place, correct the ones presenting the highest exposure
> Turn off home wifi. Hardwire the router with CAT6-8 cable, or put a kill switch to turn off during sleep. Some routers come with provision to turn down signal strength
> Shield your house from nnEMFs, its no doubt quite involving but totally worth it. You may start with your sleeping location. There are shielding paints containing graphite fibre, carbon fibre, conductive particles that earths nnEMF pollution through a ground connection.
> Shielding clothing can help a little though its not a complete solution.

Note: if its 'money no bar' for you, consider a whole home assessment from nnEMF remediation specialist.

Strategies to reduce cell phone exposure:

> Activate airplane mode when not in use, or else it pings cell towers every few minutes
> Disable other modes of connectivity when not in use. Phones have multiple antennas working, like Bluetooth, hotspot, geo location, etc switch off all.
> Turn phone off at night
> Charge your phone away from your body
> Hold it away from your ear: speaker mode is best. An air-tube headset is

second best. A low power wireless headset is third best. And just holding it away from head is fourth best. Even an inch or two can cut exposure dramatically.

➢ Avoid using laptop, tablets on your lap
➢ Avoid using phone when reception is poor: cell phones crank up signal strength when signal is weak
➢ Avoid poorly shielded cases: shielding cases for phones are rising among the wise & proactive but beware of faulty shielding which makes your phone crank up power
➢ Impact protection cases: some impact cases can increase your absorption of radiation by 20-70%
➢ Avoid using phones in moving vehicles: signal strength increases when phone switches from one cell tower to another
➢ Switch to a previous generation signal for lower power: some phones allow you to choose older communication protocols (like 3G instead of 4G) in the settings. You may not notice difference in call quality but it will reduce nnEMF signals drastically
➢ Be wary of frequency harmonizers: harmonizing low frequency waves with stickers & pendants reduces some damages but not others. Risk of cancer & neurological injury still remains.

The real causes of common conditions

Cancer:

It is caused when a person loses control over growth mechanisms, that means malfunction of autophagy & apoptosis. Its impossible for cancer to manifest when apoptosis is working properly because the immune system can tell when a cell has reached a point beyond repair. Then unrepairable cells are instructed to self destruct to make way for new cells. But in cancerous state cells are not repaired properly & also not dying off as they are supposed to, instead they are growing & dividing fast. So what causes malfunction of apoptosis leading to cancer ?

Before cancer emerges, electron transport chain is slow. Slower the ETC, less chance of you losing control over apoptosis. But two things are responsible for cancer:

> - Speed of electrons across ETC be high to support abnormal cell growth
> - Make huge free radicals that destroy mitochondrial and nuclear DNA

These two are partners in causing cancer and what fuels them both is an overrun ETC.

The ETC runs fast when there is solar deficiency. Vitamin D receptors in Cytochrome III slows down the ETC when you get lots of sun. UV-B makes vitamin D. With lots of sun you get energy directly and so ETC doesn't have to run so fast & purposely slows down the oxidative phosphorylation. Sun exposure also dilates blood vessels to absorb more UV and enhance oxygen delivery. Since UV penetrates under 1mm of tissue, nitric oxide dilates blood vessels to bring blood closer to surface. UV light puts the brakes on ETC when you start getting energy from sun and less from food. Sun is truly a nature's vaccine against cancer while low vitamin D is no.1 risk factor for breast cancer. Other factors encouraging cancerous cells:

> Deficient autophagy
> Low redox
> Weak detoxing
> Inflammation/acidity

But when ETC is prone to making free radicals, more oxygen is actually harmful. That's why the body often develops sleep apnea as a protective mechanism to starve the body of oxygen. Oxygen is useful in cases where your autophagy & apoptosis is still working & heteroplasmy rate is improving. So naturally curing cancer revolves around:

> Reducing free radicals & inflammation
> Degenerative programming
> Resulting (epi)genetic mutations

All of the above can be possible only if mitochondrial efficiency is restored. Some mito-hacks to avoid cancer:

> Correct bipolar magnetic fields in home, (spl sleeping & working space).

- ➢ Increase energy production & detoxification with strong earth-type magnetism
- ➢ Decontaminate your home of unnatural frequencies
- ➢ Get lots of full spectrum sunlight on eyes & skin, as close to the equator as possible (or at latitudes)
- ➢ Cut fluoride out of water & food
- ➢ Deplete deuterium with seasonal diet or specific protocols
- ➢ Cut down foods that acidify, increase foods that alkalize
- ➢ Do a heavy-duty detox, & continue detoxing daily

Thin hair:

hair was thick till 70s & 80s, but modern youngsters have thin hair. Chronic, systemic stress can be blamed but partly. Real cause is:

- ➢ Artificial blue light (no natural light)
- ➢ nnEMFs
- ➢ poor sleep quality
- ➢ stimulants
- ➢ psychological stress
- ➢ toxins (like fluoride)
- ➢ trauma (other stressors)

the above are the main bulk of the reasons. This affects mitochondria and finally thyroid. A subclinical hypothyroidism occurs and thyroid starts cutting back on energy wherever it can, and the hair looks like an extra luxury to the thyroid.

Electro-hypersensitivity (EHS):

It is mainly caused by 50 & 60Hz electric fields along with dirty electricity and also microwaves from our tech devices. It results in:

> - the ETC cant burn fats & proteins as well, so mitochondria uses glucose & carbs for energy.
> - Inflammation & oxidative stress
> - Increased stress response
> - Elevated histamines
> - Lower melatonin
> - Anti-myelin antibodies

And the above conditions can turn into:

> - Brain fog, memory difficulties
> - Disrupted sleep
> - Blood sugar problems
> - Headaches, dizziness, migraines
> - Asthma, allergies
> - Weakness & fatigue
> - Hearing problem, tinnitus
> - Speech difficulties
> - Depression, anxiety, irritability
> - Skin problems
> - Stress
> - Digestive disorders
> - Heart problems, high BP
> - Flu-like symptoms/breathing problems
> - Sensitivity to light/eye problems
> - Tremors, cramps

> ➢ Joint & muscle pain, numbness
> ➢ Lower sperm motility & testosterone
> ➢ Erectile disfunction
> ➢ Weight gain

As a solution you have to remediate your nnEMF environment, or else no treatment will solve the root cause. Moving out of the EMF zone often does miracles.

Autoimmune diseases:

Root cause of auto-immune diseases is a circadian mismatch between light entering the eye, and the light absorbed by T-regulator cells in the 'gut associated lymphoid tissue' (GALT) where the food is broken down. Autoimmunity starts when circadian clock in the brain (SCN) gets out of sync with the circadian clock in the GALT. In real life that translates to getting artificial blue light from smartphones, TV, LED lights in the absence of UV & IR from full spectrum sun whereas your gut is getting summertime UV light signal released from the chips you are eating. Hence the eye & gut receive conflicting signals about your light environment, so your infradian biology gets confused. As a result it doesn't know which season you are in and which program it should run. T-regulator cells of GALT basically gets blurry vision and attacks everything.

Sleep apnea:

Deuterium overload in the central brain stem which controls breathing is main cause of sleep apnea (among others). This localized toxicity impairs mitochondrial function in that place and you lose the urge to breathe. Plus the airway also get obstructed. Other factors which also contribute to this condition are:

> ➢ Poor melatonin levels
> ➢ Excessive cortisol/adrenalin keeping stress levels high
> ➢ Blue light toxicity, nnEMF exposure
> ➢ Excessive deuterium in diet
> ➢ Stimulant consumption
> ➢ Circadian mismatches

Cataracts:

Cataracts are a defensive mechanism against too much red light. Red & IR are generally beneficial but too much of it from an artificial source causes the body to defend against it by turning the lens cloudy. Also equally important to know that when doctors replace cataract, they put an artificial lens (which blocks 100% UV & 50% blue light) which make the person's health worse.

Solution: getting full spectrum sun during day, avoiding artificial light at night.

Mold toxicity:

It is caused by nnEMFs by destroying mitochondrial metabolism which makes us more sensitive to mould. So when we get our light, water, magnetism, seasonal eating right, most mould reactions go away.

Dental fluorosis:

For decades we have been taught that nothing could be done about those spots or pitting on our teeth. That it's an unfortunate side effect of fluoride, if you want it's benefit of harder enamel. Fluoridated water & toothpaste should be avoided. Tooth power based on charcoal, clay & essential oils should be used as it detoxifies, cleans & whitens better.

Cavities are believed to be permanent and beyond repair but that's not true, with right nutrients and avoiding certain insults to teeth, they can actually remineralize. Tooth building (and bone building) is like this:

> - Trace minerals needed are phosphorus, selenium, boron, magnesium, cobalt & calcium, and the fat-soluble vitamins needed to direct these minerals to right place are vitamins A,D,E & K2
> - Calcium & minerals are bricks in teeth & bones
> - Collagen, fat & protein are the mortar that holds the wall together
> - Fat soluble vitamins coordinate construction by telling materials where to go

What we are lacking is phosphorus as 'building block', collagen & protein as 'glue' and some vitamins found in animal products as facilitator. Vitamin K2 in particular tells calcium where to go, like bones and teeth, not into soft tissue like kidney, bile duct, pineal gland & eyes. Shortage of these vitamins are serious problem for vegans and vegetarians. And ultimately the driving force behind this is 'redox potential', net negative charge helps the materials go where they should. Gum disease can be reversed by sunlight exposure.

Vitiligo:

It is caused by mis-matched light hitting eyes, skin & gut. Its results in a circadian mismatch with the melanocytes that produce melanin in the skin. The solution is to reverse mitochondrial damage and following Dr Jack's protocols.

Clogged arteries (atherosclerosis, peripheral artery disease, coronary heart disease):

Doctor blame cholesterol & inflammation for such diseases because that's what they find there. Real reason is reversed polarity of blood vessel wall, which create false signal of injury. Blood vessels are supposed to be negatively charged so that negative charged blood flow freely by repulsive force, but when heavy metals like mercury & lead build up in interior vessel wall cells, the cells change polarity and positive charge is the signal of injury which calls for healing to the area. Poor mitochondrial function and shortage of ATP inhibit heavy metal removal. This mechanism was designed to heed actual injury but instead causes cardiovascular blockages and inflammation. In a study by university of Wisconsin, 120 heart attack dead bodies were checked and every one of them showed mercury and lead deposits in the areas of inflammation and plaque build-up proving this theory. Solutions are sleeping in magnetico sleeping pads (if possible) and a chelating agent like DMSA which helps remove heavy metal from blood.

Bad skin:

Unhealthy skin is caused in-part by worn-out mitochondria & intra-cellular (metabolic) dehydration. Better way to improve skin tone is from inside out with hydration, better diet, detoxification, exercise & healing the microbiome. If healthy mitochondria is added to that mix, your skin will be as beautiful as can be. Mitochondria make water to keep skin plump, smooth & youthful. That's because water:

> - Stores redox energy from sun & food in its e-zone
> - Maintains the surfaces of proteins for good mitochondria & cell function
> - Enable the skin to make vitamin D
> - Enhance detoxification

Bottom line: diet, detoxing, exercise & ingesting water are one level removed from the actual driver of attractive skin, which is mitochondria(which rocks). Moisturizers, clinical exfoliation & laser treatments are two level removed from the source of great skin. Ultimate truth is mitochondria (in great shape) makes your skin fabulous.

Biochemicals (like testosterone) gives you the joy of life:

Mechanisms that cause low testosterone are:

> ➢ Blue light/microwave (activating the adrenals non-stop)
> ➢ Circadian mismatches
> ➢ Signalling breakdowns
> ➢ Nutrient deficiencies

Testosterone modulates how men feel physically and mentally. It affects muscle building, libido, fat distribution & bone mass. It has body & mind enhancing qualities for women, but not enough for them to bounce back after hard physical labour. Low testosterone makes you feel really lousy, as if you are 'less than' & makes it a pain to go through life. The following tips can help:

> ➢ Be acutely aware of how biochemicals like serotonin, dopamine & testosterone control your feeling of wellbeing
> ➢ Improve your light & EMF exposures. See the sun rise, cut out blue & increase UV
> ➢ Fix faults that hinder biochemical production (nutrient deficiencies)
> ➢ Reduce stress levels from sympathetic activators
> ➢ Ground yourself as much as possible
> ➢ Raise your redox potential

Remember sunlight itself is almost like a one-man-army.

Finally just keep in mind that all bodily problems caused due to bad lifestyle and abuse of mitochondria are reversible, just don't give up. It will take some time but you will be rewarded for sure.

The End

Thank you readers,

If this piece of work added any value to your life, kindly consider rating this book as it will support me a lot.

Regards

Avishek Mukhopadhyay

www.ingramcontent.com/pod-product-compliance
Lightning Source LLC
Chambersburg PA
CBHW040738120726
48007CB00008B/129